Charles H. Hall

Spina Christi musings in holy week

Or thorns compose a saviors crown

Charles H. Hall

Spina Christi musings in holy week
Or thorns compose a saviors crown

ISBN/EAN: 9783741195921

Manufactured in Europe, USA, Canada, Australia, Japa

Cover: Foto ©Andreas Hilbeck / pixelio.de

Manufactured and distributed by brebook publishing software
(www.brebook.com)

Charles H. Hall

Spina Christi musings in holy week

SPINA CHRISTI:

OR

MUSINGS IN HOLY WEEK.

SPINÆ CHRISTI

MUSINGS IN HOLY WEEK

"OR THORNS COMPOSE A SAVIOR'S CROWN"

BY

CHARLES H. HALL, D.D.

Rector of the Church of the Holy Trinity, Brooklyn.

Orphan Press.
Church Charity Foundation.
BROOKLYN 1874.

SPINA CHRISTI:

MUSINGS IN HOLY WEEK,

OR,

"Thorns Compose a Saviour's Crown."

BY

CHARLES H. HALL, D. D.,

Rector of the Church of the Holy Trinity, Brooklyn.

BROOKLYN:

ORPHAN PRESS, CHURCH CHARITY FOUNDATION.

NEW YORK: E. P. DUTTON & CO.

1874.

BROOKLYN, N. Y.
ORPHANS' PRESS—CHURCH CHARITY FOUNDATION.

PREFACE.

NOTHING like originality is claimed in this manual, nor desired.
There is offered to those who may feel
the need of such help, my own ideal of a
profitable method of considering Holy
Week. Those who listen to the services
of this sacred time will see that the design
of this little volume is subsidiary to my
pastoral teaching. Easter flowers, blood-
stained from Calvary, bloom on our altars
and on the graves of Greenwood as well.
Easter joys are joys of faith over conquest
of personal sins, and personal doubts.
In the jarring discord and profane de-
bates on all these matters, religious joy, in
conscious identification with Christ, alike

in suffering and in victory over death,
seems to be the accident of a miracle or
the vagary of an enthusiast.   May we not,
as the poet Keble has given it (or must
it all be only an unreal dream), may we
not value the profound mingling of
truths personal and vital, of the Paschal
Week, because

> " duly then
> The bitter herbs of earth are set,
> Till temper'd by the Saviour's prayer,
> And with the Saviour's life-blood wet,
> They turn to sweetness, and drop holy balm,
> Soft as imprisoned martyr's death-bed calm."

As an humble attempt to make the
Week of the Passion more of a reality to
Christian people, the following plan has
been attempted.   First, to give definite-
ness (and without learned discussions)
to the events and teachings of each day—
to show where Jesus was on each day of
this week and how employed.   Was not

His the pure and perfect dying—and, is He not in it as in all, our model and ensample of how to love and trust God in life and death? Next, it is my wish to offer, in all modesty, the thoughts as briefly as possible, which may help one to connect Christ's deeds and words with "all that ancient prophets said," and, as well, with all that His Church was afterwards to say, so far as to show our personal identifiableness with Him — that we may claim Him, not only in doctrinal exactitudes of thought, but in affections— that we may lie at His feet, and feel imagination, affection, yearning—yea, 'body, soul and spirit' kindling on His altar.

The theory of the harmony of the four Gospels on which the meditations proceed, is that of the learned Dr. Jarvis.

The notes aim to manifest that certain slight variations are not mistakes—at least not unintentional.

The Church has followed another plan in the order of reading the Gospels for this week. That for Palm-Sunday is from St. Matthew xxvii., which, with the Second Lesson, St. Matt. xxvi., makes the whole scene of the Passion to pass before us. For Monday and Tuesday the Gospels contain the same account as given by St. Mark, chs. xiv. and xv. On Wednesday and Thursday St. Luke follows, chs. xxii. and xxiii.; while the beloved Apostle concludes the direful story on the anniversary of the great crime. It was perhaps something more than poetry in the Fathers of the Church to dwell on the coincidences of symbolism in Scripture. But it is singular, that the order of the standards in the camp of

Israel; of *Reuben (north), Judah (east), Ephraim (west), and Dan (south), and the order of the faces of the cherubim guarding the throne of Jehovah in the visions of †Ezekiel, which was the same; and the four living creatures of the Apocalypse as they appeared in 'the midst of the throne'‡ on which was the Lamb—(of old attributed to the four Gospels—as guards and exponents of Redeeming Love)—should fall into one and the same position, as they raise for us the solemn Trisagion of Holy Week. St. Matthew—whose symbol, like Reuben's, was the man, speaks first: the standard of Judah, the lion of St. Mark, follows: the writer for all men, who told the story of a Sacrifice made for all, St. Luke (with Ephraim's sign, the ox) takes

---

* Numbers ii. 10, 3, 18, 25.
† Ezekiel i. and x.   ‡ Rev. iv. 9-11.

the days of betrayal and of the Supper ;
and the eagle-eyed St. John (see symbol of
Dan) sits nearest the great Mystery—to
break the power of remorse at the crime
with the pitiful accents of pardoning
love. The story of the love wherewith
God loved the world and gave His Son
for its life, needs this fourfold telling,
that all that is within us may praise the
Father, Son, and Holy Ghost.

INTRODUCTION.

SIX days before the Passover, as we suppose on Friday, the 19th of March—and some time after the raising of Lazarus, Jesus returned to Bethany, where Lazarus and his sisters were living. These faithful friends made a feast for Him, and Mary—not of Magdala nor the 'woman who was a sinner'—but the 'one who had chosen the better part' in the purity and integrity of her virtuous womanhood, anointed Him unwittingly for His burial.

The Pharisees forecast that they must put Lazarus out of the way, as they hear of this supper.

The Sabbath (from Friday at sunset till Saturday at the same hour) intervenes, when on Sunday—not a day of rest to them, but their first working day—Jesus

inaugurates the triumphal procession,
which ends with the cross.   Ezekiel (ch.
xliii. 1–6) had foreseen this great ap-
proach on its divine side, when he beheld
the Glory of the Lord coming from the
way of the East ; His voice like 'a noise
of many waters ; and the earth shined
with His glory.' We see it on the human
side—and faith pictures the other—and
utters to Him the echo of that first day
of palms—Hosanna in the Highest !

Read carefully in the following order :
Matt. xxi. 1–11 ; Mark xii. 1–11 ; Luke
xix. 29–46 ; John xii. 12–19 ; Matt. xxi.
12–16 ; John xii. 20–50.

CONTENTS.

The Sunday next before Easter.

"Rejoice greatly, O daughter of Zion ; shout, O daughter of Jerusalem : behold, thy King cometh unto thee :
He is just, and having salvation ; lowly, and riding
upon an ass, and upon a colt the foal of an ass."—*Zech.*
ix. 9.

> "Ride on! ride on in majesty!
> In lowly pomp, ride on to die :
> O Christ! Thy triumphs now begin
> O'er captive death and conquered sin."
>
> DEAN MILMAN.

LENT draws again to a close, and the
record passes into our last account.
The Great Week, or Holy Week as it

---

* It is meant by this change of numbers that our common
numbering is in error by six years : that A.D. 34, when
these events occurred, was really 28 : when, as we know
the moon's position and the vernal equinox, of course we
know the days of the year on which the Passover came.

has been called for ages among Christian
people, has come round again. In the
days of St. Chrysostom men everywhere
abstained from business and gave themselves up to prayer and fasting, and deeds
of mercy in pardoning or helping.
Kings and emperors often set the example of unusual charities—as is seen
still in the rites remaining on Maundy-
Thursday. Should we not leave the
world for a season—to give up a little of
our own time to meditation on the
Passion of our Lord—in which all sad-
dest and all most joyful facts and thoughts
meet together, by Divine appointment,
for our discipline and blessing. Thoughts
of death cross thoughts of victory. Palm
branches are borne by crowds of weeping
expectants—children's voices sing in the
temple Hosannas, that mingle in with
the lament over Jerusalem. We look
down the dark avenue of the valley of
the shadow of death, and see the form
of One like unto the Son of Man where

the shadows gather the thickest, and hear
the wail, "Father, forgive," and feel in
our hearts that the pardon may reach us.
Holy Week puts forth in all its gospels
and epistles, its symbols and hymns, the
great paradox of the Christian faith—of
death in life and life in death. It is the
One great lesson of the Church's year.
As the Lamb of God took our nature
upon Him, and being found in fashion
as a man, was obedient unto death, even
the death of the cross—so He died for
our sakes—He led captivity captive, that
we should be free from sin and fear, yea,
from him who hath the power of death—
the Evil one, ever seeking by the tempta-
tions of the world and the flesh to hold
us back from walking now with the Lamb
in His sorrow, lest we should walk with
Him hereafter in joy. Mercifully grant, O
God, that we may for a little give up the
world and follow the example step by step
of that divine patience, that we may also
be made partakers of His resurrection !

Palm Sunday—or as in the ancient Prayer Books it was called *Dominica in ramis Palmarum*—opens before us the two extremes of Christian doctrine—faith anticipating victory by death. The Son of God, Lord of lords and King of kings, yet meek and lowly, and riding on a poor beast—emblem of humility and lowliness—He comes in state!

> " The angel armies of the skies
> Look down with sad and wondering eyes !"

Pharisees and zealots behold with angry looks, and minds exacerbated by all the symbols, which they too well understand, and say within their hearts— "The Nazarene must die, and not all the people perish." And every deed and word, reader, is for you and me. This week we pass now, and Good Friday and Easter, if God's holy inspirations may be allowed to control us, may speak to us "winged words," to fit and prepare us for a day when we are to die—by such faith as we have in these scenes; when we are to rise again—by the power and at the call of this humble Rider. Bend thy thoughts to this sacred pathway along the valley—count over its steps and find the rifts in the Rock of Ages—against the time when thou wouldst fain find wells of salvation in the valley of weeping— and trust that for thee it is to be made real : that these holy weeks well spent have then fitted thee for one final great week— when buried with Christ in the baptism with which He baptizes the pure in heart, thou shalt rest in Him.

Palm Sunday was the first working day of the Jewish week in which came the fourteenth Nisan—the Paschal feast. And on this day they brought into the city and up to the temple gates their chosen lamb, carefully selected out of the flocks, "without blemish, a male of the first year, taken out of the sheep or the goats" (Ex. xii. 3, 5). The priests must inspect them and pass judgment ; for there must be no spot or mark, no disease or falsehood—no trick nor mistake, and many circumstances would occur to cause anxiety. Behold them ; and call up in fancy the motley throng, as they pass on. They have streamed as rivulets out of the villages of Galilee, and passed over the Jordan near Tiberias and avoided hated Samaria. Other parties have joined them from the wooded slopes of hither Bashan, and where the Jabbok leaps down its oak-clad ravines, by the spot where Jacob saw the double hosts of the angelic ministers of the Lord. They come from the land of Gilead, where once David fled for refuge, and in whose secret hiding-places other believers shall yet be concealed * for love of David's Son. Now in the early morning, after the rest of their Sabbath is ended, they are seen thronging the tracks which lead to the city. One stream of people appears coming up towards Olivet, and

---

* The Christian Jews fled from Jerusalem to Pella during the siege.

passing through Bethany; and Jews of
all the East probably gathered in that
current—on foot or mounted—poor villagers of Galilee and rich traders from
Damascus, and Palmyra, and far beyond,
where men dream of the Ophir and
Havilah of old—ignorant shepherds who
come to sell, with the choicest of their
flocks before them; and wealthy scholars
who are dwelling still where Daniel ruled
and Ezekiel saw visions under the "terrible crystal" of Chaldea — who were to
buy themselves a lamb for the sacrifice.
All Israelites whose fathers had once
been roused at the midnight call of that
Egyptian passover, fifteen centuries before this, felt the thrill of this annual
memorial. The sun shines clear and
warm on the slopes of the Mount of
Olives, as Jesus leaves the lowly home
of Lazarus and his sisters, and mingles
with the travellers. All men mused of
Him. The rulers are armed against Him.
Months before this He had called

Lazarus from the tomb. He had then vanished from the public eye, and had spent the time in Ephraim beyond the Jordan, "and continued there with His disciples"—(*St. John* xi. 54). Thus starting, as it were, from the tomb of Lazarus, He now goes willingly to His own! In the recall of the one to life, we see the link of unity with His own resurrection.

He is the Paschal Lamb. All shadows and human scenes of inspired life meet in Him. Behold Him taking thought to fulfil the prophecy of Zechariah : "Fear not, daughter of Zion! thy King cometh, sitting on an ass's colt." In this lowly pomp, and possibly along this same winding track, Solomon had ridden "on the King's mule, on his way to the valley and Zion, to receive the kingdom of David, and the anointing of Zadok the priest. We may suppose that the former. scene suggested itself to some persons in the throng about our

Lord. "See, he fulfils the words of Zechariah to the letter! He comes as came Solomon,* when hateful foes conspired against him. Lo! he has chosen thus to come. ● He sent His servants for this 'colt whereon never man sat.' He is meaning at last to be King! Down with the Gentiles! "Hosanna to the Son of David! Hosanna in the highest!" As formerly "the earth rent with the sound of them" who welcomed Solomon (1 *Kings* i. 40); so now the sound of the shout is heard far down to the valley of the Kedron, and goes before them till "the whole city is moved," at this last expiring burst of a nation's mistaken zeal

---

* See 1 *Kings* i. 33. "Cause Solomon my son to ride upon mine own mule and bring him down to Gihon." The Rabbins tell us that it was death for any one to ride on the King's mule, without his permission, and thus it would be more evident to all that the proceedings with respect to Solomon had David's sanction."—*Smith's Dic.* "The Targum of Jonathan, and the Syriac and Arabic versions have *Shiloah, i. e.*, Siloam, for Gihon. The anointing of Solomon took place probably in or near the valley of the Kedron—across which our Saviour passed.

and patriotism. If Jesus had intended to rule as other kings, the crisis of His career had now come. The people, galled and weary of Roman rule, felt one great quaver and storm of joy at the thought of Him, and then woke to deeper hatred and capabilities of rage against Him, at the bitter disappointment of their hopes.

Children's voices take up the cry. Solomon, like Samuel, had been the loved example with Jewish mothers ; for he had been a wise and dutiful son to his own ; and doubtless the children caught the meaning of the cry of their elders, and the broad area of the temple is noisy with the unusual sound of "children's voices answer making" of Hosanna to the Son of David ! Our Solomon ! our Prince of Peace ! While they rejoice that the dawn of that great kingdom of the Messiah had come, and exult in it, He whom they laud and honor is found weeping, as the city comes in view. Pharisees ask of Him to restrain the people, and to them He replies, "that such was the force of facts upon them, and such the plain fulfilment of prophecies, that if men should be silent 'the very stones' would immediately cry out." But He knew the mystery of sin—how that seeing, we see not; how we are borne on a current, and even as we seem to see the shore before us, the tides sweep us away, and turn us to other things. He weeps over Jerusalem—that she has fallen. She has not known her *day*, and its warning hours are passing. Before His prophetic eye lay the encompassing trenches of the Roman soldiery, and all the fearful vaticinations of Moses, whose bitter fulfilment was now pressing on.—Read *Deut.* xxviii. 15–68.

Unmoved by human ambition and with regal equanimity, the Son of David fulfils the double part of this Palm Sunday. He enters the temple of his Father, whither He had once come as a boy of twelve to accept His citizenship, and had called it then *His Father's house* * in opposition to His mother's speech, "Thy father and I have sought thee sorrowing." As King and ruler then, He cleanses it, against the great Paschal Feast. Again, as He had done at the beginning of his public ministry (*St. John* ii. 13–23), He went into the temple, and "*began* to cast out them that sold therein" (*St. Luke* xix. 45–46).

He also, to the eye of faith, presents Himself as the true Paschal Lamb. The people approve Him as the fulfiller of prophecy.† The temple receives Him as

---

* See *St. Luke* ii. 49.

"The Sinaitic MSS. has, 'that I must be in my Father's house.' The word *business* is not in the text but is supplied. Literally it would read, 'that I must be in the —— of my Father.' But in any way taken the *ta tou patros* refers certainly immediately to the temple, is the visible dwelling-place of the invisible God."—
OLSHAUSEN.

† "Now, therefore, prophetic figure was in truth ful-filled, when Christ was led as a lamb to the slaughter, by whose blood, sprinkled upon our door-post, that is, by whose mark of the cross signed on our foreheads, we

its king; and as He speaks to his disciples and the multitudes and to certain Greeks who had sought Him, of the common longings for immortal life and the way which leads to it through death—(the argument of St. Paul afterwards, *Comp. St. John* xii. 24 and 1 *Cor.* xv. 36)—with troubled cry He appeals to heaven against man's ingratitude. God speaks to Him from heaven — so that "the people that stood by said that it thundered. Others said, an angel spake to Him."—(*St. John* xii. 29.) Then uttering the great doctrine of His Mission, He declares that the hour of doom had indeed come—that 'He would be lifted

---

are saved from the perdition of this world, as the Israelites from the Egyptian slavery and destruction, and we make a blessed passover when we cross over from the devil to Christ, and from this unstable generation to His kingdom of most sure foundations.—*Col.* i. 13."

ST. AUGUSTINE.

"It was ordained by God that not only the Old Testament ceremonial of Divine worship, but also the historical records of the people, were to form types of higher spiritual phenomena, viz., of the economy, doctrine and history of Christianity."—OLSHAUSEN.

up from the earth and would draw all
men unto Him.' And bidding them
value the light and walk in it, He departed and did hide Himself from them.
He returned to Bethany by the same
path which He had followed in the
morning.

Easter, in order to be ours, must be
looked at as opened for us, through the
death of Christ—through our death—and
through the *death of sin in us.* These
ancient rites and types must be translated
for us into the heart's own language and
adopted in the life, till we practice all
they mean and require. Waste not life
in the outer portals, O my soul, of seeing
only in the past, as one sees a drama,
what has been done by another. What
great capacities of power and goodness
have been wrought out of a sensitive manhood, all keen and thrilling with life
and tenderness! Look not on at a distance, nor work only as unreasoning

pathos may incite thee. Press up to the meek Rider and learn of Him how to offer all thy affections and powers to the Father, and to pass unmurmuring and unterrified to die. He was troubled, and His soul became sorrowful unto death. Men wondered at His grief, and vainly offered to comfort Him by promises of faithful courage with the sword. But He paused not.—"For this cause came I to this hour. Father, glorify Thy Name." So there will be a time with most Christians when 'the hour' will come to each one in turn, when worlds cannot weigh in value with that calm faith, which then puts down all fear of death. Let it come now to thy fancy. Lift death out of its gloom, and look at it calmly. Kindle on it God's gracious resplendency of promises, by these Holy Weeks. So pass, as one with Christ, along each day, that you may 'die unto sin' anew, as He died from all evil here, and with new vigor, arise unto righteousness and new-

ness of life. Leave not this divine
wisdom to the last and weary days of
life. To be a Christian is to accept all
Christ's positions and conditions—all His
states and deeds, as well as His precepts
and orders—His sorrows as well as His
joys—His cross before His crown : in a
word to be *like Him*, till in thine inner
soul 'He is born in thee, the hope of
glory.' It is not enough to read about
Him, to hang delighted over the heroic
story of His victory, to melt in pity at the
agony or start in pleased wonder at the
fulfilment of prophecy in Him. We must
go with Him. "Let this same mind be in
you which was also in Christ Jesus," which
is the Epistle and key-note of this, as St.
Jerome called it '*Indulgence Sunday*,' " *ut
indulgentiam percipere mereamur*"—that we
may win pardon ; or as the commentary
of St. Gregory has it—' that we may begin
to find our way to that great largesse of
God—the redemption of the Lamb
which was slain.'

COLLECT FOR PALM SUNDAY.

"Almighty and everlasting God, who of thy tender love towards mankind, has sent thy Son, our Saviour Jesus Christ, to take upon him our flesh, and to suffer death upon the cross, that all mankind should follow the example of his great humility; Mercifully grant, that we may both follow the example of his patience, and also be made partakers of his resurrection; through the same Jesus Christ our Lord. *Amen.*"

Monday before Easter.

March 22. True Era, 28.

"And He was clothed with a vesture dipped in blood; and His name is called, *The Word of God.*"—*Rev.* xix. 13.
"Thou that killest the prophets and stonest them that are sent unto thee."—*St. Matt.* xxiii. 37.

"Dear sacred haunts of glory and of wo,
Help us, one hour, to trace His musings high and low,
One heart-ennobling hour!"   KEBLE.

Read first, St. Matt. xxi. 18, 19; St. Mark xi. 12-19.

BETHANY was a hamlet lying on the eastern slope of the Mount of Olives. The traveller, after passing through it and then by Bethphage, rises slowly, till he stands on the top of the ridge of Olivet, with the chief crest of the hill on his right above him and a

lesser eminence on the left. Spread out
before him is *El-Khuds* as the Arab calls
it to-day, the Holy City; its lowest part
nearest to him, and the western sides
rising gradually to the wall and towers
of Phasael and Hippicus on the west.
A small cannon planted on the hill-side
where he stands could probably reach
every spot of this city : the eye can take
it all in at a glance. Below is the temple *
area—about 1200 by 1900 feet on the
south-east corner wall ; in the centre of
which was the temple of Herod, shining
in the morning sun with its covering of
yellow gold; around it the broad area of
El-Haram, bounded by the porches of
Solomon and the costly buildings which
excited the exultation of the disciples.

---

* "The triple Temple of Jerusalem—the lower court
standing on its magnificent terraces—the inner court
raised on its platform in the centre of this—and the
Temple itself, rising out of this group and crowning the
whole—must have formed, when combined with the
beauty of its situation, one of the most splendid archi-
tectural combinations of the ancient world."—*Smith's Dic.*

On its northern limit, joined by stairs, was the castle of Antonia, the military heart of the city. Behind it, and rising higher, was Zion, "beautiful for situation, the joy of the whole earth;" on the sides (or slopes northward) of the north, is "the city of the great King." Toward the north-west, the land rose gradually, where in our Lord's day a second and third wall encircled and protected the weaker side of the city. There rises to-day the Church of the Holy Sepulchre—not on *Mount* Calvary, for there is no such mountain or hill, except in the dreams of poets who knew no better. Calvarion— the skull-place—was a single rock, about fifteen feet high and thirty feet over the top, on which the three crosses would appear with frightful prominence. Thus the entire city lay exposed to the eye of the traveller, and there is sad eloquence n the fact, that Jesus wept over it, from iis plain vision of its temple, its palaces d homes, and His yearnings went out for it, as if He would shield it from the impending destruction. We shall have this view again in Holy Week.

On Monday, in the early morning, our Saviour was in the act of descending the hill to enter the temple and spend the day in public ministrations, when He saw "a fig-tree * afar off, having leaves "—and came to it, in hunger, as any wayfarer might, if haply He might find anything thereon, for the time of figs was not yet. He found nothing on it but leaves only, and, as St. Mark seems to intimate, did not expect to find it otherwise than He did—a poor, unhappy braggart fig-tree, which had anticipated the season, and, by a freak of nature, stood as a *lusus naturæ* and false show on the sunny slopes of the hill.

Infidels have wailed in their pity at the loss of this fig-tree, refusing to see that it was used by Christ for a sublime pur-

---

* Margin, " *one fig-tree,*" *i.e.* standing alone and prominent.

pose, and has become the means of conveying a truth of wonderful clearness and force. Jesus said to the fig-tree, "No man eat fruit of thee hereafter forever." * St. Peter, the next day, as he saw the fig-tree "dried from the roots," called to remembrance these words, and spake of it as a *curse*, or imprecation. And why not, even if we look only at the tree? If barren and forced, and false to the laws of its kind, was it not likely enough (to answer any of our cavils) to be radically defective, and a monstrous growth, and fit only for destruction? But looked at as an example and illustration, printed deep in the memories of the disciples, to be the more easily remembered by its startling rapidity of ruin, and to be recalled by them, when the awful fulfilment of its loss came round in the final destruction of that which it symbolized, the boastful and fruitless city of the broken cov-

* *Matt.* xxi. 19 ; *Mark.* xi. 14.

enant, from which no man was ever again to gather fruit unto peace and holiness ! Immediately this tree began to wither. Of a hot March morning in Palestine, after a softening dew, with a hot sun rising rapidly, and drying the cool night air, the progress of wilting would be rapid enough to be plainly visible in a very short time. Before the party left the place they saw signs "presently" of its doom.

They went on their way to the city, and again Jesus 'began to cast out them' who profanely made His Father's house a house of merchandise. This trading was done in and around the Court of the Gentiles, for whom the Jewish rulers entertained no great charity or respect. The animals used in the sacrifices were to be found and purchased there ; and other wandering brokers, as we read, after gathering the coins used at the temple, in all parts of the world, brought them thither and sold them to their brethren at a usurious advance, making it, in our Lord's judgment, 'a den of thieves.'—*St. Mark* xi. 15–18.

It is easy to see why the Scribes and Chief-priests sought to destroy Jesus, fearing and hating Him as they did, because 'all the people were astonished at *His doctrine.*' He spent his day then in *doctrine,* or in teaching the people ; 'a lamb in the midst of wolves ;' and 'when the even was come, he went out of the city,' and returned to Bethany, as a temporary home.

The great event then of this day, as it lies in the inspired record, is the cursing of the fig-tree. Let us note that the *curse,* is only a divine permission to follow its nature ; as it was barren, to continue barren ; a type * of that lovely city,

---

* " Origen saith that this fig-tree was a tree representing the people of the Jews. This was a living fig-tree, and therefore heard a curse suitable to its condition ; therefore the synagogue of the Jews is unfruitful and shall continue so, till the fulness of the Gentiles doth come in."—*Whitby.*

then seeming so fair under the morning
sun ; and thus a type of every hapless son
of Adam who loses the season of his probation and yields no fruit in holiness of
character.

It was a symbol of the city and nation.
No words could tell the story more exactly. The mind recurs, perforce, to the
parable which had prepared the way for it.
St. Luke says nothing of this tree, but he
alone has given the parable of a fig-tree,
whose owner coming to it for three years
found no fruit thereon. It cumbered
the ground of his vineyard, and must be
cut down. But lo, the vine-dresser
plead for one more trial of its powers,
that he might use all means of help for
it, before the axe should be laid to its
root. If after that effort it should be
found barren, then 'thou shalt cut it
down.' It was not difficult for the disciples to see His covert meaning in the parable. They can hardly miss the parabolic
signification now. For three years Jesus

had been seeking fruit in yonder city, spread out below them, and found none. What must be its fate with a just God, who makes all things *work together*, and has fixed in nature a law, that the barren and false are always nigh to destruction, so that they may make room for the fruitful and the true!

It was a common thing with the prophets to liken the nation to a vine or fig-tree.   Instances of the vine as a parable occur in *Psalm* lxxx. 8, and *Isaiah* v. 1–7 ; and of the fig-tree, in *Hosea* ix. 10 : "I found Israel like grapes in the wilderness ; I saw your fathers as the first ripe in the fig-tree at her first time." Over the Beautiful Gate of the Court of the Women in the Temple, was the symbol of the vine—rich with the gifts of all the tribes, because of their pride in this prophetic imagery.   "Amidst other nations they appear as especially noble and destined to work great results ; but their abuse of privileges, granted them

by the free grace of God, caused them to
fail of producing spiritual fruit ; they fell
from their vocation and lost their talent.
Yet for them also did the Saviour go to
death, and time must yet be given to
disclose the effect of preaching His
suffering and death. But since even the
fire of this preaching did not melt their
hearts, the people fell under the awful
judgment of God. The history of Israel,
however, is a type of mankind generally,
who are called to spiritual life, and in so
far the parable is to be referred to the
great community of the Church, and its
final judgment."—OLSHAUSEN on *St.
Luke* xiii. 6–9.

So now all the woes denounced by
Moses as from the Ebal of cursings to the
Gerizim of blessings in that awful twenty-
seventh chapter of Deuteronomy, which
with its two sides of the covenant of
life or death, was destined to stand as
two lofty eminences about the fearful con-
tingency of their law, were gathering

over the doomed city. The Lord was "bringing a nation from afar, from the end of the earth as the eagle flieth," and siege, straitness and famine unparalleled, deaths innumerable were drawing down over that city, all because they would not observe "to do all the words of this law that are written in this book, that they should fear this glorious and fearful name, THE LORD THY GOD."— *Deut.* xxvii. 58. The Divine types and shadows had gathered over Israel and Jerusalem, and they are consistent to the last. The justice which allowed the bolt to fall, was the same beneficent law which removes the barren for the fruitful —the false-seeming and hateful for the useful and beneficent. "The land which beareth thorns and briars is rejected and nigh unto cursing; whose end is to be burned."—*Heb.* vi. 8. And why not?

Let us on this day keep to this law of the divine working, and meditate upon it.

First, as bearing closely on us personally, in the records of all the sacred symbols. Every believer loses a powerful stimulant to virtue and hope, who refuses to study carefully God's peculiar language of symbols, types, and dramatic dealings with men and nations, which, not satisfied with one act or person, are pregnant of signification to all who study them.

Our knowledge of our life and death, of that mystic law which underlies all things, which is revealed in the changing seasons and generations, as one dies to make way for the next, to rise upward to the next; of God's infinite glory, of His will with us, of rest in the grave, of the secret stone which shall be our password by the gates of Paradise, of the mysteries of pardon, is exceeding small, if it is to be confined to orthodox *prosaic propositions* of bare intellect. If God indeed speaks to us, all possible faculties in us are concerned in the sacred message, and all are exhausted in trying to spell it out.

Imagination, affections, combinations of
the entire 'body, soul and spirit,' from the
highest reason to the lowest act of worship,
are necessary, yea, all assert themselves
in a true, vital and engrossing faith
in things belonging to life and death.
So the Church is His Alphabet of living
signs : the covenants are as a harp,
touched by His hand, and all the strings
vibrate with the supernal music. Yea,
what are we doing in Holy Week, but
calling on all our nature to help us ap-
prehend the meaning of Christ's death,
and so of ours, the mystery of when we
touch Him and He touches us by the
aid of no one faculty, but of all—of body,
soul, and spirit; of keen logical understanding, to grasp the precise lines of
thought and measure the exact angles of
vision ; of the warm affections, to cleave
to what is lovely in Him, who somehow
saves us by love ; of ardent imagination,
to bring the Man of Sorrows before us as
living, as just there before us, in the spot

"where the shadows darkest fall;" of even the body, that by fasting and bowed head and knee, alone and in church, we may fall low in the dust and call on Him to be near us, to convey to us, as it were, the touch of His healing hand— above all that combination of all these, with Conscience and the Will, by which our greater vital resolutions are always made, which we call *faith* *—because it is not one faculty—but a living whole of all that is within us, all taking all circumstances—of frequent prayer, alone and in public, of harmonious exhortations to seek for a present Saviour, so that while past times, and old Catholic usages are crowding and pressing on us, and lifting us, we may condense all, and if but for an instant get a glimpse of Him who died for us; who will be at our side when we die in Him, whose voice will be as familiar to our ear as it

---

* *Fides formata*—faith made perfect through love.

was to that of Lazarus, when it was heard by him in the bosom of Hades, saying, "Lazarus, come forth !"

Now the typical languages and sacred hieroglyphics of that one city, Jerusalem, from the first sacrifice of Isaac down to this day of its last fearful symbol, the barren fig-tree, are as perfect in grammar and accidence, as the simplest tongue on earth. "These things are an allegory"—*Gal.* iv. 24 ; "Now these things happened unto them for ensamples (*types* in the margin) and they are written for our admonition on whom the ends of the world are come"—1 *Cor.* x. 11 : "For whatsoever things were written before, were written for our learning, that we through patience and comfort of the Scriptures might have hope"—*Rom.* xv. 4. They help us to a knowledge of God's laws over us and in us, and demand all our faculties to grasp them.

On the rocky summit of "one of the mountains of Moriah" the early faith of

the Patriarch Abraham had been *tested*,
whether he would dare to give up his
dearest thing for God, at His word; and
he obeyed, even to dare to put death
between himself and his only beloved son
Isaac—"accounting that God was able
to raise him up, even from the dead,
from whence also he received him in a
figure"—*Heb.* xi. 19. And faith then
'saw the day of Christ' and was glad—
knew what that *day* meant, and how God
would give, as He had asked, and would
set forth His own Son in sacrifice as
the propitiation for our sins.

On that temple hill, the Ark of the
Covenant, pregnant with meaning to
Israel and all mankind, had rested from
its long journeys. There, before the
mercy-seat, Cherubim had supported the
symbol of the inner vital life of the
nation, its faith in God's presence with
them. Types, and figures, and dramas
and tragedies innumerable—idolatries of
false gods and avengements by the true—

psalms of sweetest celestial melody, far
beyond man in their origin, and horrid
perversions of all man's nature—David's
reign and David's sin—Solomon, Josiah,
Nebuchadnezzar's relentless armies—fire
and sword, then silence and ruin, and
then slow gatherings back to life—a
smaller temple; a weakling band, boast-
ing of their "never in bondage," but
really never quite otherwise—and brave
Maccabean priests and heroic sufferers—
the story of that sacred spot is the great
story of man's struggles for a knowledge
of God.   There we go, and as we muse,
all that we know of God as revealed to
us, as saving us, comes charged with its
series of prodigious events.   And if our
efforts in Passion-week can, by our
prayerful industry, help us to reproduce
and make real to us the presence of God,
as in that temple, first in cloud and fire,
and then in 'form as a man,' be sure we
need all such helps as the Church gives
us ; freedom from worldly care and

pleasure, time to think, time to recall
the great drama which moved through
the first *great week*, time and prayer and
faithful meditation on the Scriptures,
that Christ may be seen by the eye of
faith, as very near to every one of us, and
saying, "My child, come and learn
from me, for I am meek and lowly ; take
up the cross and follow me."

The days of superior inspiration have
passed ; for the faith was once for all delivered to the saints, and that sublimer
inspiration would now only be adding
to the record of the faith more than we
need by every word it uttered. But what
the Spirit once taught, the Spirit must
now reveal to us ; and it leads us now
up to where we feel the beat and impulse
of that lofty power of *vital faith*, when
God touches us as He touched them, and
a vision is vouchsafed of the WORD OF
GOD—as a living being to us—as our
King and guide unto death. "Who is
this that cometh from Edom, with dyed

garments from Bozrah ; His garments sprinkled with blood ?" May we not have a sight of Him in our degree. May we not look through type and symbol, and behold Him, even as St. John saw Him : ''And on his vesture and his thigh a name written, King of kings and Lord of lords." ''Lo! I am with you alway!" Only let faith have her perfect work. It is not her perfect work simply to rectify opinions, or to accept the ethical decisions of the past. She can draw us nearer to a living Christ, if we, as other good men have done, will do all that is given us to do, and work with all our faculties to bring Him near.

Sacred are the hours of this Holy week. We draw near, by the call of the Catholic world, to the cross. Does not the very air become heavy with the wings of angels and the messages of love, electric with meaning, as the gorgeous clouds gather about us, of the living forces of a living God !

Let us look at the blasted fig-tree, and learn our duty to 'know in this our day the things that belong to our peace,' to leave awhile our lower worldly life, and stand with Jesus on Olivet, and cleanse for Him the temple of our hearts, that He may come in, and abide, and touch us with His love. Death now swallows up all life that fails of its end and feeds on all that is defective and false, that itself may yet be swallowed up of life. A dead, cold faith, which sees only a barren life of theory, and mopes and mutters around a vacant tomb, is useless. Christ must touch all our nature with the healing of His hands ; and as He did on this day 'heal the lame and the blind,' that we may rise and see Him, as showing us how to die to sin, and thus to have no fear beside.

"So when Time's veil shall fall asunder,
  The soul may know
 No fearful change, nor sudden wonder,
 Nor sink the weight of mystery under,
But with the upward rise, and with the vastness grow."
                                    WHITTIER.

COLLECT FOR SIXTH SUNDAY AFTER EPIPHANY.

O God, whose blessed Son was manifested that he might destroy the works of the devil, and make us the sons of God, and heirs of eternal life; Grant us, we beseech thee, that, having this hope, we may purify ourselves, even as he is pure; that, when he shall appear again with power and great glory, we may be made like unto him in his eternal and glorious kingdom; where with thee, O Father, and thee, O Holy Ghost, he liveth and reigneth, ever one God, world without end. *Amen.*

Tuesday before Easter.

March 23. *True Era,* A.D. *28.*

——"when ye depart out of that house, or city, shake off the dust of your feet."—*St. Matt.* x. 14.

> " But the deaf heart, the dumb by choice,
> The laggard soul, that will not wake,
> The guilt that scorns to be forgiven ;
> These baffle e'en the spells of heaven."

TO-DAY ends the public teaching of 'our Lord, and the day of offered grace to Judah and Jerusalem. When the multitudes see Jesus again, it is as a prisoner and victim ; then as silent before them, as now the opposite ; then returning no word to the 'contradiction of sinners' against Him.

A solemn awe gathers over the mind of a reader of these parts of the Gospel, as he sees the Great Teacher bending

Himself with earnest effort, to a fruitless effort, persuading them with all His faculties, with a wisdom which, knowing all that is in man, also knew what was before the crowds of sinners to whom He was speaking, and saw 'His own hour,' and, beyond it, theirs ; His cross on the stone of Golgotha, and theirs, innumerable almost in 'the valley of slaughter' between the city wall and the trenches of the Roman legionaries. Yet, His public teaching ends with a wail, as sitting on the hill of Olivet, He murmurs His mourning over the city of David. Lo, O my soul ! the God who created this world for thy probation, has given thee the fearful power of 'seeing, to see not, of hearing, to hear not ; of moving in scenes of redeeming love and using the means of grace, and yet disappointing thy Saviour of the love and obedience of thy soul ! Flee from thine hardness and impenitence of heart, and hear the word which comes to thee from this day,

sounding down the ages as the alarum-
bell of the city of the saints—*Vigilate,*
watch—

> " Watch, as if on that alone
> Hung the issue of the day,
> Pray that help may be sent down ;
> Watch and pray !"

The day begins with the seeing of the
fig-tree 'dried up from the roots.' Inci-
dentally this tells us that the day had been
clear and warm. The sun looked down
from a cloudless sky ; the moon, near its
full, shone out of a serene expanse. Nature took no part in man's passions ;
undisturbed as the voiceless cherubim, at
the gate of the garden of Eden, who kept
unceasing watch and ward over the path
to the Tree of life. The long sunny
hours of Monday passed, and the tree
shrivelled and dessicated, but the citizens
yet in their green tree took no heed of
the dry, or what should be done in it.
In a manner this day is all illustrated by
this dry tree. Jesus is seen as a Master in
Israel, seeking fruit on every branch, of

Scribe, Pharisee, Sadducee and Hero-
dian—all—and finding none, and then
denouncing, as He had before done to
the tree, woes, on the hypocrisy which
shut the gate to the kingdom of heaven
against men.   He comes back to the
Mount, possibly sits near this blasted fig-
tree, and sketches the dark days of vengeance 'such as had not been' nor should
be ever again in ordinary history.

St. Matt. xxi. 20–22 ; *St. Mark.* ix.
20–26.

Jesus and the disciples came in from
Bethany, passing near the fig-tree mentioned the day before.   He uses it to
point His day's work : ' if ye have faith
and doubt not' all things are possible to
you ; you shall have all things which
you need.   He is throwing His arms, as
it were, about them, before their hour of
trial.   As they on Saturday stand there,
and look to the north-western corner of
the outer wall, where is a tomb holding

all their hopes, the mountain itself may murmur back to them, 'if thou hast faith, this may be removed,' what means it—oh wait my soul—what means it. So to thee, reader, *faith* is not arbitrary and without limits, but is credence in God's word, in what God has commanded. If thou hast faith in these holy scenes, and in thine heart dost ask for help, it will come to thee, and the mountain of care will remove, if, as Jesus did, thou learnest to forgive.

St. Matt. xxi. 23–27; *St. Mark* xi. 27–33; *St. Luke* xx. 1–8.

Jesus was 'walking in the temple' and was 'teaching.' The word *temple* has in these writings two meanings; sometimes it is the shrine proper or *nave*, the small building in the centre of the space, where were the altars and the holy chambers. At other times, as here, it signifies the whole area, in which it was usual to congregate for any purpose. It is plain

that the Jewish magnates had so far ma-
tured their plans of hostility, that they
had determined to worry Jesus into saying something of an unguarded nature,
which can justify an appeal to the courts
either Jewish or Roman, and allow them
with some show of justice to destroy Him.
Hence the first portion of this day is a
scene of dialectical skill and craft on one
side, of simple enunciation of truth on
the other.   Many questions existed of
a delicate nature.   It was easy to offend
the rulers, easier to rouse the sullen passions of the Jews, easiest to say, what by
their traditions might seem wicked and
impious.   They *came upon* Him, or made
a dash at Him, saying, 'Master, tell us
by what authority doest thou these things?'
It was skilfully put.   Jesus shows His
appreciation of their subtlety, by avoiding it.   He does not answer.   *Any* reply
might have been tortured to false uses.
He asks them, in return, pointing at the
same time to His great witness, ' whence

came John Ben-Zacchary ?   If He was a
prophet, he told you whence I draw my
authority.   If he was not 'of heaven,'
settle it with the common folk.   They
say, 'we cannot tell '—nor would He.

St. Matt. xxi. 28 to xxii. 15 ; *St. Mark*
xii. 1–12 ; *St. Luke* xx. 9–19.

Jesus advanced on their line of battle,
with parables.   Parables, prophetic symbols and hieroglyphics were a definite
language among the Hebrews.   Things
were thus spoken by living pictures,
which could not be said in ordinary
words.   So here—two sons—one very
pious in speech, evil in action—the other
wrong in word, but truly penitent, repre-
sent the chief relation between Him and
the classes of hearers always about him.
Hear another, of a householder, and his
vineyard—the slain servants—the son at
last standing in peril from their brutality
and ingratitude, and meditate on that old
prophetic word ' of the Stone set at nought

of the builders.' The woeful style rises
in force and grandeur, of a king's son,
and his marriage—strangely treated by
his subjects, and despised by one of them,
who lacked a marriage garment, and was
speechless, to show that *a call* is not *a
choice.* A sitting at the 'feast of fat things
and wines on the lees' here, does not
insure indiscriminate favor hereafter.

St. Matt. xxii. 15–46; *St. Mark* xii.
13–37; *St. Luke* xx. 20–44.

The Pharisees withdraw and take counsel, and try again. They tested Him on
the side of the common people and the
law; they will now try the side of the
Roman rulers. There is jealousy and
savage vengeance enough in such men as
Pilate, if they can only mould it to their
wish. Behold this double deputation,
'strict Pharisees and loose Herodians'—
oil and water in amity. How soft the
little doubt slips out. How smooth the
compliment ! 'Tell us of *tribute* to Cæsar.'

Again Jesus shows their skill by His own; He would not answer a query so fraught with sore points of feverish prejudice—a *denarius* gives the answer. "They marvelled at it and went their way."

The enemy sends in an assault from the left flank. The Sadducees are roused and try their hand with a difficulty, whose answer was not as dangerous to political peace, but which may serve its purpose as well, if they can trip Him up. Master, seven men and one wife—in the resurrection, how is it? Jesus does not answer them point by point, or their subtleties would have come into play; but goes back to the common instinct of man, and touches the deep undertone of our yearning for immortality. God is the God of the living, and all live to Him.

Once more and from another point a Pharisee, admiring this reply, so unlike all that his own school had made, puts to Him, the great perplexity of rival schools—then and since—Which is the grand, atoning piety of all? This question Jesus answers directly, for He saw that the 'discreet' scribe "was not far from the kingdom of God."

While they are together, Jesus returns on them with one question—of David's son called by David "my Lord"— humble as a son: with some mystery in His nature as Lord, sitting on the right hand of God—how could it be? They in their turn dare not make any answer, nor from that time ask Him any more questions.

St. Matt. xxiii. 1–41 ; *St. Mark* xii. 38–44 ; *St. Luke* xx. 45 ; xxi. 4.

Jesus turns to the common people and utters to them His last Discourse. Obey your rulers as sitting in Moses' seat, but forget not the difference between their words and works. The Woes which are pronounced seem to echo against Ebal and Gerizim, as they show how thoroughly the nation had lost justice, judgment and truth, and had filled up the measure of their fathers. "Ye serpents, ye generation of vipers, how can ye escape the damnation of hell?"

The half shekel tax to the temple for its oil, etc., is being paid. One poor widow brings hers, and it signifies a day's fast to her to save it for the purpose; and our Lord seems to seize upon it as a drop of refreshment and true grace, after the past excitement. His last words are of infinite pity, but none the less fraught with sorrow: 'Ye shall not see me henceforth'—till the last scene of all— that is, as your voluntary teacher and Messias. As victim they did see Him, but not after His resurrection.

St. Matt. xxiv. xxv.; *St. Mark* xiii.; *St. Luke* xxi. 5–36.

His public voluntary life and teaching are done, for now He is *to be led* as a lamb to the slaughter. Jesus departs from the temple. The disciples admiringly point to the magnificence, which dazzled their provincial imaginations; as if exultant that such a glorious centre and Keblah of their future royal kingdom should be there. What amazement smote on them as the Master rejects it all! What has happened to Him! He has just now confounded His foes. Why does He turn against the religion of His tribe?

Four of them come to Him, as He sits apart on Olivet, looking down on the city, and ask Him what it means. He chants to them the solemn *Dies iræ, dies illa*—not so much as sung by David and the Sybil, as by Moses, in the solemn, minute and terrible denunciations of Deuteronomy (ch. xxviii). It is the strain taken up again by the one whose awful response is heard in the chapters of the Apocalypse. Thus these two, Jesus sitting on the Mount of Olives (symbol of peace) and St. John the Divine sitting on the * Mount of Exile, looking off to the clouds gathering over the blue sea, chant for all ages the requiem of nations, of worlds, or of souls, where the light has gone out, and the true life has turned to falsehood, wrong and crime. Dark storm-clouds pass over the scenes which tell first the fall of Jerusalem in that generation, of Rome and the old Babylonian-born civilization in a few more centuries; and in both indicate the final conquest of the "Stone hewn out of the mountain without hands" over the kingdom of evil. This chapter formed the litany of thought of the future apostolic age (See 2 *Thess.* ii.), and its key-note of *watchfulness* belongs to the Church to the end of time.

Three great parables, rising one over the other, conclude this day's wondrous teaching.

---

* There is a grotto on the south side of the island of Patmos, in the hill which overlooks the sea, which tradition has fixed on as the scene of the apocalyptic visions.

I. *St. Matt.* xxv. 1–13.   The Church is like ten virgins expectant—some wise and thoughtful, some giddy; some churches parochial, national; some souls are watchful, full of prompt, living works, ready for the coming joy; others, in all respects like them to the eye, ruined are by carelessness.   Watch ye therefore, all.

II. *Ibid.* xxv. 14–30.   It is as a man going away and leaving a threefold charge—one, five and ten—and bidding all improve the trust while he is gone. At his return will be the compensation to all who have had faith in him absent, enough to work for him as he bade them. The principle of that compensation is indicated as "grace upon grace to every soul that believeth": self-horror, outer darkness and irremediable grief to the profane.

III. *Ibid.* verses 31–46.   The Shepherd-king gathers all nations before Him to judgment, and all individuals come in their own forms, as they rise. They who "have attained *the* resurrection" appear as the Lamb in white, and take their places, and hear the deep echoes of their faith in confessed likeness to Jesus ; that they had caught His spirit and been like Him. The others, hirsute and rejected in their own record, turn away to eternal fire prepared for the devil and his angels. Thus, this day puts before us the offer of life and death.

St. Matt. xxvi. 1–13 ; *St. Mark* xiv. 1–9 ; *St. Luke* xxi. 37, 38.

Jesus goes out to Bethany, and being at supper in the house of Simon the leper, there came to Him for the third *

---

* There were three such scenes : 1. The first was in the house of Simon the Pharisee, by a woman ' who was a sinner,' *Luke* vii. 37, etc. 2. The next was six days before this Passover, in the house and by the sister of Lazarus, *John* xii. 1–3. This was two days before the same, in the house of Simon the leper, and by a woman unnamed. Poor Mary of Magdala, who figured in neither, has been

as from a human standpoint He looks on
His approaching end.   We hear the Prophet, or Messiah, as one, and speaking to
all doubters to "trust in the Name of
the Lord and to stay upon His God," for
all His enemies shall be only as sparks
and soon destroyed.

The same identification of persons between Christ and believers, this inspired
confusedness of style, which sees both in
one, is the warmer tone of the Christian
life.   "Christ is in you, the hope of
glory."

Is it an object of desire, that we should
so far grow up to this style, that we can
observe Him on this Tuesday night, in
this hamlet, and after life's weary fitful
fever ended, to learn ourselves to

" dread
The grave as little as our bed " ?

Is it desirable ? The lives of Christians
answer in the negative.   Death is made
gloomy and kept afar.   We are willing
to be like Christ in prosperous things, in

popular things, in the joys of Eden and raptures and visions of hope ; but we resolutely keep off and mourn at the approaches of any painful similarity. But, my soul, is there not for thee a last Tuesday in Holy Week? Is it not well to see in fancy thy last day's work done ; the actual accomplished ; the last effort made, and then to turn slowly and ah ! how painfully round, and look at the cross, which may not be avoided ; which will not away one day. See the believer of our common sort. The physician has been called, after untold struggles in secret, and has looked at the little spot on the bosom, or has sounded the chest, or has felt the pulse, and we look to him so anxiously, and he pitifully shakes his head, and consigns us to this night of Holy Week. Ah, how do we weep and sink in terror, that our lives are mortal. Come, trembler, and see how quietly He sleeps, who has all day long been breasting the waves of hate and suspicion and profane unbe-

lief; who has worked for three years to
win His countrymen to Him, and ah, how
few points of comfort were there in His
Tuesday!   His disciples, were they
pleased that woes were to come on them
and their temple? One woman cast in
two mites, and Jesus saw it, and was re-
freshed in heart by it.   One woman
poured her gratitude at His feet, and its
perfume soothed Him more than the
ointment.   And now, if we should have
such a day of ended work, would we not
wail over a defeated and disappointed
life!

See Him as He sleeps, after His work
of life.

> "The last, the fiercest strife is nigh:
> The Father, on His sapphire Throne,
> Awaits His own anointed Son."

Do you say that a sense of His divine
nature kept Him from your weakness.
"He was tried *in all points like as we are*"
—in none, more thoroughly than the fear
'ath.   It is by a false treatment of
 that we rob ourselves of comfort

here. Ye too, if ye have escaped the corruption of the world through lust, are partakers of the divine nature, and by the gift of your faith, are one with Him ; and if ye believe in your hearts and doubt not, ye can say to any mountain ' Depart.' Voluntarily, by loving identity; by prayer to God to do to us no better, to love us no more, and treat us in our degree by no other rules than He treated Him ; and then kissing His footsteps, measuring us by His outstretched arms, following Him wherever He goes, *by our will*, as we may by faith and prayer; *by His will*, as we can by patience and obedience wherever He leads us ; we may draw on our faith for needful courage. Many a man escapes the natural fears of death, who does not avoid the mistakes of sectarian notions.

These services, as we follow Jesus, are able to bring Him very near, if we are wise and diligent. They teach us how to look more gently on death, and ' walking in darkness' to find in the Name of

the Lord, in the habits of mind and
heart which are thus produced, a reason-
able religious and holy hope.'

> " Christ leads me through no darker rooms
> Than He went through before ;
> He that into God's kingdom comes
> Must enter by this door."

The room is not very dark in Bethany.
Let us meditate on it, and so use the
means which are given us, that we may
rest when we come to it, as come we
shall, in peace with God and in charity
with the world.

Wednesday before Easter.

March 24.   True Era, A.D. *28.*

"The ransomed spirits one by one were brought
To His mind's eye —— two silent nights and days,
In calmness for His foreseen hour He stays."

KEBLE.

" And as it is appointed unto all men once to die, but after this the judgment ; so Christ was once offered to bear the sins of many."—*Heb.* ix. 27, 28.

THE words "Now *before* the feast of the Passover" fixes the date accurately of the Supper, which is mentioned in the thirteenth chapter of the Gospel of St. John, and the conversation at which is continued to the end of the next chapter, and concludes with the words, "Arise, let us go hence."   As the evangelists did not write with any marked human skill, there are of course any number of objections to any plan of fixing dates for them—and the weaving of a plan and the demolishing of all others going before has occupied the minds of scholars in this department, in every age. We give a period which seems natural. Supper was generally taken after the day's work was ended. There would be no such meal preceding the paschal feast, so that a supper before the Passover naturally places it on the preceding evening after sunset, which was *Thursday* in their week, as their day *began* at sunset. The scene of this meal was probably at Bethany, and possibly "the end of our Lord's intercourse with the family of Lazarus, the next being spent with the apostles alone."*

Of the day itself until sunset nothing has been related. It is not proper for us, in the lack of definite knowledge, to attempt to fill up the silences and gaps of Scripture with our conjectures. We left

* J. H. Blount.

our Lord on the preceding day in the
house of Simon the leper. We cannot
say that He did not again attempt to
move the minds of the inhabitants of
Jerusalem, or, that what is given by St.
Matthew is not the compendium of His
teaching through this and the next day.
But we find Him again on this evening—
and the act of humility, the sweet charity
and peace which breathe in His words,
are indicative of entire serenity, as if He
had been somewhere alone, and gathering the forces of mind and body for the
awful tragedy before Him.

They err, who confuse the manhood
of Jesus with His divinity. He suffered
as man, and touches our nature at all
points, sin only excepted. We pity Him
and sympathize with Him in His tenderness and weakness, as a man. The lamb
none the less feels the crushing teeth of
the lion, that it is fair and pure. He
who denies Jesus a man's fear of dying
by the cross, loses all the power of His

divine sympathy in return.   "He offered
up strong crying and tears unto Him
that was able to save Him from death."*
Thus was He like us.   We may go with
Him step by step, on these Holy Week
scenes, to prepare for the days when we
shall ask Him to go with us.   So we
seem to see Him gaining the rest of two
quiet days, and first going in mind and
fancy through the scenes before Him.

First we have the scene of His humility.
He rises from supper, and washes the
disciples' feet.   In that region of sands
and arid wadys and dry hills, where men
used either rude sandals in walking, or
nothing, the native courtesy was to minister to this necessity.   The custom was
apparently general to provide this means
of refreshment.   The slave was probably
the one to whose lot it usually fell.   If
this supper was in the house of Lazarus,
probably his poverty may have prevented
him from affording the party this atten-

---

* *Heb.* v. 7.

tion. What a surprise to them all, intent as they were on the actions of their royal companion, to see Him, not begin to organize armies or provide them the plan of a coming campaign, but choosing the place of a slave.

When a year before they and others had offered to make Him a king ;* Jesus checked and quieted the fever of ambition by sending them alone on the Sea of Galilee in a night storm, and coming to them 'walking on the water.' Now, as no words of His can persuade them of His spirituality of intention, a *deed* must do what it may for them ; if not to open their eyes, at least to remain in their memories after He was gone. We coolly wonder at their blindness and slowness of heart to believe. How is it with us ?. Just beyond that little line, our friend is in Paradise. Do we practically accept it ? Just beyond another point, the gate meets us, where the narrow path runs

---

* *Luke* vii. 44.

into a momentary darkness, and stretches
away into pure light beyond.   Do we
lay it to heart, and use our Easter priv-
ilege to cast out all fear, in a blessed
hope that maketh not ashamed?

Peter, ever impetuous and full of noble
natural zeal for the "things that are seen,"
will not be washed, lest the king to be,
may be for an instant dishonored; and
next rushing, as was his wont, to the
other extreme, will have more than is
offered; on neither side catching the
deeper meaning, that Jesus would have
him give up his imperial dream and be
converted into a child, that he might
have part with Him.   "If I wash thee
not thou hast no part with Me."*   The
act of His love must touch them all;
and, when its true meaning came out,
after their eyes were at last opened, they
would see that they must maintain that
humble mind, if they would be clean
before Him.   He resumes His clothes

---

* Compare *Matt.* xx. 25–28.

and explains to them the action. "If I your King, have done this to you, be slaves in all good deeds to your brethren, and hold nothing to be too low in loving-kindness when done for Me."—"Whosoever will be chief among you let him be your minister."

This loving strain suddenly jars with the sense of the presence of the traitor, who was doomed to realize the prophecy of a deed, which nature abhors : to press down on the bosom of the man of sorrows the keen thorn of ingratitude ; to betray the Master with whom he had ' eaten bread.' No washing can make him clean, whose faith in the divine ideal of love is quenched. Possibly the faintest sneer touched the bended lip of Judas, as he saw this curious act of servility. How far he had gone, only Christ and he knew—but, even then, we suppose that a group of men were waiting for him to consummate his full bargain of blood-money, at the house of Caiaphas. He

is yet cool and self-poised—and as they
ask in horror, at the suspicion of treachery, *Is it I?* he too is no whit behind
to follow suit. Is it I? Peter bids John
ask who is the offender, and why? Did
he feel the rising of that just anger against
the secret traitor which all might have
had to some purpose, if their dream of
a military king had been true!. It sur-
prises us, at first sight, that so little came
of the question; that when Judas had
gone out with Satan in his heart, they
knew not "for what intent He spake
this unto him;" but deemed, most
simple folk, that as he had the bag, he
had gone out to provide something
"against the feast," or give something to
the poor. Judas hastened to the chief-
priests and arranged, what alas! for him,
had been 'predestined to be done from
the foundation of the world.' As he
leaves Christ at the friendly board, sacred
in all eyes, pagan or Jewish—so he will
seek His ruin and find Him again in the

sacred retreats of the garden, where, as Judas knew, He sought the presence of God, and thus complete an act whose guilt is unparalleled. The love of money, and the god of this world, were the ruin of Judas ; the carrying the bag of this little company, small as its contents probably were, and meagre as could have been the ' defaulting,' had proved too much for his nature. As Clement says, the perfect or complete Christian of his age understood the mystery of the fourth and sixth days of the week (Wednesday and Friday, which were called by the names of Mercury and Venus,) and, so fasts all his life from *covetousness* and lust, meaning that these were the peculiar vices of Mercury and Venus, among the nations; so the Christian may still find some of the 'open secret' of truth in the usage which has commended itself to all ages, to mark the day of the betrayal as a day for common litany, to be delivered from covetousness. One paints Judas as a black-browed, heavy and ill-looking traitor. Why then did not all at once point to him ? Why did they not discover him when Jesus gave him the sop ? Alas, no. Possibly he was the smoothest and in all recognized sympathies with popular piety, the most righteous-seeming of that little company. He loses the moral of his life, who sees not the Judas in his own soul, which feels the dangerous glitter of money and the pomps and vanity which money can compass, which may stir even as the serpent in Eden, and delude the soul to its fatal downfall. Were vice always that 'monster of hateful mien,' and *seen* by us as it is, we might have needed another form of many an 'ensample written for our sakes;' but, on the very reverse of the poet's line, we sin with our eyes looking only to the loveliest forms of thought, and look back to see the blackness of our deeds when it is too late.

Why and how Judas fell, we seek not to exactly determine ; we may more profitably ponder the fact that *Wednesday* in Holy Week leaves its echo in every week, even the wail of the litany, pleading against the sin of covetousness which is idolatry : "From all inordinate and sinful affections, and from all the deceits of the world, the flesh, and the devil, Good Lord, deliver us." The Church early recognized the fact, that Judas sinned as representative of *man*. Could the Judas-element have been taken out of his race, there had been less doubt about Christ. Jesus would have called crowds to His feet. Could it be taken out of us, we should believe on Him quickly. Therefore, as we can conquer it —the love of this present evil world—we can accomplish the work of faith, and overcome the fear of death. Why do we cast longing, lingering looks behind us, as we are seen to go, but that we love the things that are seen, and feel the coldness and vagueness of our faith in the things unseen. Judas in us pleads for rest—for the green fields of the valley of Siddim ; and will not see that worldly prosperity is full of pitfalls and evil, with fires rolling beneath, and great storms impending.

Let us look now into the company from which Judas has gone out, and see how the Master, in whose heart was no taint of inordinate affection, prepared to die. We are so to use our chief, religious services, that we may see the reasons why He had no undue fear of dying : and how we may be like Him. Surely, of them all, these Holy Weeks fail to help us, if they do not bring us face to face with One who died for us, that we in turn might die to the evil world and put down the carnal heart of unbelief. Therefore, on thy knees, oh, my soul, look on thy Saviour as He walks the descending valley, and know that thou too art soon to follow thither. Mark each step where

He places His feet, as the Alpine traveller watches the descent of his guide, and note them well. When thou dost indeed follow, thine eyes must be turned heavenwards as His were, and then well is it with thee if the memory of these essays help thee by the 'reflex action' of pious contemplations to tread warily the dangerous pass.*

To us on the hither side of the cloud which separates this vale of tears from the serene abodes of light, the treachery and ingratitude of Judas, thus stabbing his Master to the quick, seems only utter darkness. It seems no strange recompense, that the horror of it afterwards brought down upon him. But there is another side which we may look at,

---

* It is well to note as a difficulty confessed, in harmonizing this passage of St. John xiii. as I have done, that I prefer to consider the verses 36-38, as *proleptic*—said in advance of the time: and to explain the words, "the cock shall not crow," as, in a general sense, it shall be before a cock crow or dawning. There are other modes of explanation which are not discussed here, because such discussions only confuse us.

namely, the relation it had to the discipline of the Son of Man, and its effect in preparing Him for giving up the life which then warmed His frame. God calls few to die suddenly, in the full vigor of life. It must be a powerful poison or violence which enters a living man and crushes the central power of physical life. Generally the race are called to walk a descending plane, to the line where the cloud shuts the farther world from sight. In this descent there are prepared checks of progress, and gentle disseverances of the cords which hold one to earth. As we see in persons led away by phthisis, there are days of conflict, and then days of rest; times when the soul braces up its energies to flit, and again, a relaxation and pause, for prayer and gathering wisdom ; so in the spiritual, there are similar checks and balances. Judas had been typified in Ahithophel—and the psalms had been strung to the wail of David at ingrati-

tude. Jesus had chanted this wail in the
service of the temple, and mused on it
in the silence of the midnight air ; and
thus as Samson ' out of the eater brought
forth meat' for His own last journey.
Doubtless as God He foresaw all that
would come to pass ; but we claim to
regard His perfect nature as man, need-
ing what we need and comforted by the
psalms as we are comforted. The act of
treachery knelled His own death. It
was a bitter cup to Him, but, ages before
it, Judas had been foretold and illustrated, and faith in God taught Jesus,
that it was only good ; that as a father
chastiseth his children, so God was
preparing Him, was easing His burden,
was leading Him into a land of preci-
pices and death, but that from everlasting
it had all been prepared and was certain
to end in victory. The act of Judas cut
some of the cords of the loving heart—
and after the cutting, it was easier for it
to break. Doubtless in another world

we shall see that even as the light of day
changes slowly and reddens with a non-
actinic light as evening draws on, so the
life of the Christian usually fades gently,
and darkness is made easier, and thus it
comes to pass, that "He giveth His
beloved sleep." Demas played such a
part to St. Paul. St. John, when he
could write himself "your companion in
tribulation," could begin to see visions
of the Church of Paradise.   If this be
true, is there not a medicine in it for us ?
As we turn down the hill-top of vigorous
life, how easy, how common is it to
complain at ingratitude, to praise the
past, to mourn a "light and loveliness"
that have passed away ; to exaggerate
hurts and obtrude wounds and bruises—
to lament inattentions and slights, to
point to great injuries and resent neglect
and injustice.   It is the folly of the
natural heart.   True wisdom teaches us
to claim by right no better lot than the
life of our Saviour—to ask to be saved,

not only by. Him as a Prince—but as He was led and purified. If the 'gall and bitterness' of the traitor's deed was not given to Him arbitrarily and for the sake of a scene—but predetermined by the Father of all as necessary to His perfected example—then all these lighter sorrows and regrets of advancing age, these neglects and slights, these pushings from the rude and bold, these shadowed, darkened paths of sickness, instead of being subjects for the unfaithful reason to murmur over, are to us the very

"stairs
That slope through darkness up to God."

If ye bear them patiently, "the spirit of glory and of God resteth upon you."

When Judas went out Jesus was relieved, for he says, "*Now* is the Son of Man glorified." The evil leaven was removed—the paschal teaching begun. "Little children, yet a little time I am with you." He bids them love one another, as the sign by which all men should know them to be His disciples.

He speaks of the many mansions or resting-places of His Father's house, the
calm abodes of Paradise, into which
He goes now to prepare a place for them.
The way to that house of God they all
knew (if they only would), as it led them
down to the tomb. We say now in
rhythmic exultation, of it :

"Since Jesus hath lain there, I dread not its gloom."

But they did dread it, and would not
understand Him ; but with Thomas
said, "How can we know the way?"
Jesus will not force down on their strug-
gling emotions the hard truth ; and
speaks to us all, in speaking to them :
"I am the way, the truth, and the life.
No man cometh to the Father but by
Me." The *way* in question here was,
the how to die, and pass to the true life.
The deep meaning is that in Christ we
learn it all—the way of going step by
step after Him; the truth of all truths in
being like Him ; the Life eternal and
begun now, over whose calm current

death, as it were, brushes away a dark cloud, and it runs in sunshine forever.

Jesus teaches them the finality of all spiritual knowledge of God in a holy life; even as a multitude of discordant voices are drawn one by one, into perfect harmony with the great key-note of all truth, and, vibrating with its music, leave nothing beyond to be desired. Therefore, when their finite wills come up to the Christ-like mould, all that they ask of God in His name 'He will do,' until in their hands greater works than any they have seen shall be done, in glorifying God. Just there, when our wills are bowed and turned to that of Christ, and our nature is exalted, comes in the great Gospel promise which removes the sting of death, which gives the mourner patience, and supports the departing with exulting hope. "If ye love Me, if ye obey Me, I will pray the Father that what has been mine shall be yours"—'and He shall give you another Comforter, abiding with

you forever, the Spirit of truth in you—
My spirit and gift—and making us one ;
separating you from the world, and giving
you My peace.' "Let not your heart be
troubled, neither let it be afraid." I am
in the act of leaving you. In a few hours
all will be over. I tell you all this, that
when it is come to pass, ye may believe.
Arise, let us go hence." We have
here a discourse of Jesus; with its beginning in the sigh of relief as Judas
left ; its great theme, and its ending, as
when with almost another sigh, at the
resistance offered by their "slowness of
heart to believe," He concludes, "Arise,
let us go hence." The day is done—the
day of separation to such as will love this
present world—of groping up to the
truth by all who love Jesus, to which
you and I, reader, are groping now;
that we ought not to fear to die, or
gather only gloom as we think of it;
that Jesus is the Way for us to learn the
Truth of eternal Life. Let us use these

days, that we may apply our hearts unto wisdom; as the Collect has it, "to that holy and heavenly wisdom whilst we live here, which may in the end bring us to life everlasting."

O Almighty God, who into the place of the traitor Judas didst choose thy faithful servant Matthias to be of the number of the twelve Apostles; Grant that thy Church being alway preserved from false Apostles, may be ordered and guided by faithful and true pastors; through Jesus Christ our Lord. *Amen.*

Thursday before Easter.

14th Nisan. March 25, A.D. 28. True Era, 34.

" Ye do show the *Lord's death.*"—1 *Cor.* xi.
" Bread of the world, in mercy broken,
   Wine of the soul, in mercy shed,
By Whom the words of life were spoken
And in Whose death our sins are dead."
                                   Bishop Heber.

THE actions and conversations of our Lord and His ten disciples during this day (Peter and John being absent in the city) are not recorded in the Gospels. We may well believe that the solemn hours were spent among the shady retreats of Olivet, in duties of prayer and religious counsel, in order to prepare Himself and them for the impending events. For Him, as for all dying men,

" These Border-Lands are calm and still,
  And solemn are their silent shades,
  And the heart welcomes them until
  The light of life's long evening fades."

All the thoughts. whioh come over a devout mind concentrate on these Paschal days, from that great night of the Egyptian Passover, when under the bright, still moon, Israel heard the shrieks of woe to alarm them to hasten away from the land of bondage, to this night of sorrow and infinite anguish, under the full moon. The Holy Supper, which tells over and over the Lord's death linked into all lives. Gethsemane, the celebrations of Holy Church, the last Communion to each one of us, when in the chamber of sickness, the white-robed minister bids us, "Take, eat, in remembrance that Christ died for *thee*"—these are the Border-Lands, and if we be wise in our cultivated habits of devotion, we may come to them, not scourged by necessity as galley slaves, but with a calm and holy courage, and find Jesus, never so

near to us as then.   "Dearly beloved,"
says the pastor to the sick one, who has
come to these

> "Shades where the living and the dead
> Look sadly in each other's faces."

".Whatsoever your sickness be, know
you certainly that it is *God's visitation.*"
How often would the reply come back,
"Yes, His visitation, in anger, in punishment." How hard it is for us so to combine our Maundy-Thursdays and all they
mean to us, with our chastisements, as
to feel by holy instinct that it is the visitation of the God of heaven, in mercy
and love, even as a father pitieth the
child of his anxious affection.

Let us first follow the two disciples
Peter and John into the city, whither they
go to make ready for the paschal Supper.
They are bidden to find the place by an
apparent *accident.* This was probably
done to prevent Judas from knowing
beforehand, and so communicating to
the priests, where the place was to be.

As the two disciples enter the East-gate of the city, they find a man bearing a pitcher of water, from some one of the fountains or pools about the hill of the Temple. It was the usage of the day, to hold things very much in common on these festivals, so that no citizen of Jerusalem would be surprised at such a salutation as this: "The Master (*i.e.*, the Teacher) saith, Where is the guest chamber, where I shall eat the passover with my disciples?" No name is given. Perhaps the man knew them; perhaps He did not wish the name to be spoken: the authorities had before this commanded that no one should receive Him. The seeming mystery may have had a simple explanation. Jesus determines to be undisturbed during this last solemn religious service, and probably no one was able to forecast His movements. The fact that Judas knew where to find Him, at the time he sought Him after the Supper, reveals His habit of visiting

Gethsemane during Holy Week. Judas is not able either to leave Him or betray Him before this passover Supper : for one custom of this ordinance was, that the lamb which was to be slain, was put forward to the priest, with the number and names of the party who were to eat of it. Any hesitation or offer at absence by Judas before the Supper would have roused suspicions of him. May it not be that this fact of his being compelled, in spite of himself, to violate no ordinary custom, but even the great passover of God, in order to betray his Master, may have afterward awakened his horror and remorse at seeing how Satan had driven him beyond all common limits of treachery and ingratitude.

The preparations for the Supper were not very extensive, but they would certainly occupy most of the day, as the lamb was to be slain "between the evenings," or between three o'clock in the afternoon and sunset. The two disciples found the man bearing a pitcher of water. They inspect the place of meeting, "a large upper-room, furnished." They buy the lamb, and use some care and trouble in selecting it, for the law has been very particular as to its kind, "without blemish a male of the first year (*Exodus* xii. 5; compare *Leviticus* xxii. 19–21). They must obtain the un-leavened bread and wine, and the bitter herbs, and prepare for the roasting of the animal. After the evening sacrifice, at three P.M., they offer it, and await the coming of their companions.

On that evening the sun sets over the empty tomb at Calvary, and the paschal moon faces it from the heights of Olivet, as the company of disciples gather to the great national feast. Exultant themselves in all its proud recollections, they wonder probably at the gloom which depresses their leader. We see Him now to have been God of God, and Light of Light; but they saw Him as a man and a Ruler destined to bring deliverance unto the tribes of Israel. Why does He bow down under a burden of sorrow? Does He suspect *us?* We will go with Him, and 'dare all that a man durst do.' Thus they reasoned. *We must* go back of the clue which is in our hands now, and see with their eyes, in order to comprehend *them;* and then, if warned by their perplexity, we look forward to our own dullness and doubts, we may find that we are all along doing the same.

We suppose this Supper to begin at eight o'clock in the evening. They had fasted since noon, and now reclined, as the Mishna says the true Israelite should do, "like a king, with the ease becoming a free man." When the first Israelites *stood* to eat the Passover they were slaves. They are now in their own land of rest. The leader, or father of the family, begins. He asks a blessing on the feast and also on the first full cup, which is in His hand. The bitter herbs are placed on the table and a portion eaten. The unleavened bread is passed around, and the lamb is brought on. The second cup of wine is filled, and one representing the son of the family asks the meaning of the feast (See *Exodus* xii. 26). The father replies and explains the record contained in *Deuteronomy* ch. xxvi. 5, and the first part of the Hallel * (Psalms cxiii., cxiv.) is sung. The lamb is carved—care being had that no bone is broken, and eaten by all who are present. The third cup of wine, and a fourth are taken. Then the second part of the Hallel (Psalms cxv. to cxviii.) is sung. A fifth cup was used, probably only in later times, and the Great Hallel sung—Psalms cxx. to cxxviii.—and the meal was at an end. It was then considered to be proper to bring on the table anything in the way of a dessert. †

---

* Shortened from Hallelujah. It was not ordered by the Law. The second part of it is supposed to have been the hymn mentioned by St. Matthew xxvi. 30.

† See *Smith's Dict.*, on the word Passover.

Thus ended that celebration of which Moses had said, "It is the Lord's Passover" (*Ex.* xii. 11), and "it shall be for a sign unto thee upon thine hand, and for a memorial between thine eyes; that the Lord's law may be in thy mouth : for with a strong hand hath the Lord brought thee out of the land of Egypt"— (*Ex.* xiii. 9). Just as the new Covenant grew out of the old, so this feast made way for another, which absorbs all that was in the older, as the young plant in growing takes its life in the old root and buds and bears fruit.

But first we may dismiss the traitor from this sacred company. Two of the historical gospels have placed the words spoken to Judas by our Lord, as having been said before the Lord's Supper, and the third, the gospel of St. Luke, which inverts this order, has in other instances done the same thing. And while neither Matthew nor Mark says that Judas went out at once, to complete the wicked deed on which he was bent, it is surely more natural for us to suppose that he did so, as some time would be required by him to accomplish his wicked purpose. As the necessity of being at the Passover had now ceased, we choose to think of this first great celebration of the communion, out of which all others spring, as freed from the presence of the traitor.

Jesus took of the bread lying before Him—and by the law of Moses only unleavened bread could be eaten at this time—and brake it with blessing as the new rite in which the Passover and its covenant ended. As the phrase had always been common to the Israelites in their celebration : "This is the Lord's Passover"—in the blood of a lamb slain : so now it is, "This is My Body which is given for you, do this in remembrance of Me." On the door-posts and lintel of the soul, yea, on the body of man, must be found the marks of this 'Lamb slain from the foundation of the world,' that the angel of vengeance may stay his hand of punishment at the sight. He took the cup, which in this feast was always wine mingled with water, and blessed it, saying, "This cup is the New Testament (*i. e.*, covenant, but a covenant *sealed with blood*. See *Hebrews* ix. 15–22), in My blood, which is shed for you and for many for the remission of sins. All of you drink of it," and they all drank of it. "Verily I say unto you, I will drink no more of the fruit of the vine, until that day when I drink it new in the kingdom of God. I am the True Vine and my Father is the husbandman." Then follows the divine discourse, which is recorded in chapters xv. xvi. and xvii. (as far as verse 26th) of the Gospel of St. John.

Alas, the infirmity of human nature ! They are contending who shall be greatest in an earthly kingdom, on their way to Gethsemane, * the valley of woe to them:

---

* We would insert in *Luke* xxii. the 39th verse between verses 30th and 31th.

and Jesus is telling them of His kingdom
as spiritual: the kingdom of the regenera-
tion, wherein were to be twelve thrones
and twelve judges of the twelve tribes;
where the laws of judgment were to be
laws of spiritual truth, and the reward, the
wine of life, to be found forever at His
table in the presence of the Father.
Then Jesus, passing out with them, goes
to the scenes of His betrayal and death.
His voluntary ministry is ended.   His human life, so far as His personal will
guided its circumstances, is given up to
the keeping and guidance of Him, who
had sent Him to die for our common sin.
To our mortal vision it seems as if nothing could explain the sublime prayer for
the unity of the Christian world in God,
and the agony and ignominy which followed.   But seen as the angels look
down on it, what lesson has man to learn
of more immediate practical wisdom than
it teaches Him; even of a power in us
to pass from 'the breaking of bread,'

along the heights of prayer, with a soul sustained by the *viaticum* of all ancient truth and divine covenants; and filled with love for the 'vine of God's planting,' to find death to be only the natural process of a new birth into a spiritual body, even the mystical body of the resurrection.

Infinite disputes seem to be the price of any just apprehension of the profound meaning of the Lord's Supper, as if Satan, like Beelzebub in the vision of John Bunyan, recognized this as a gate to life, and planted his forts and archers over against its portal. We would avoid all angry feeling in these days of personal effort after truth, and offer a word or two, as far as may be removed, from strife.

1. No one text seems to hold the whole revelation of the Spiritual Presence. Therefore no doctrine is all true which does not take in all texts, and all irresistable inferences from such as are entirely comprehended ; hesitating at inferences

from those only in part comprehensible. To illustrate this principle, we may refer to an instrument which excites our admiration. To study the processes of the photosphere of the sun, men now use an instrument which is composed as follows: On the arc of a circle a system of lenses and mirrors are arranged at proper angles of reflection and concentration, around the fragment of the circle, until such a quantity only of the intense light of that dazzling planet is received in the last mirror of the set as may be safely and carefully observed and studied. A proper telescope is placed so as to observe this resultant figure of the sun, and the student now looks steadily upon his face, and detects the story of each hour and minute of his fiery life. Thus, in one instance, a variation was seen, by which a stream of light occurred, through a space of two hundred thousand miles in an interval of only ten minutes. If all this complex contrivance be necessary to enable us to gaze on the created sun and read his deeds, is it too much to claim that a combination and careful adjustment of all the texts and luminous helps of the intenser life of the Church are required, to aid us to see the face of the Sun of Righteousness, and not be blasted by the intense splendor.   One may shut his eyes to the sun of day, and walk in darkness.   One may deny all supernal meaning in the Sacrament that binds earth and heaven, and focuses on a corrupted and sinful world the sacrifice of Calvary.   He also walks in darkness, and most lonely darkness, when he prepares to go away from the communion of men.   There are due limits of the truth, in any such synthesis and collection of the inspired sayings, to avoid superstition ; but there must be such charity toward minor differences, as to allow us each to study at this system of lenses and mirrors, so that truly and in every deed we may communicate with Christ, ''both God and man;" and to know that we are "very members incorporate in His mystical body," and heirs now of a consciousness that may smile at the terrors of death.

2. Again, imagine a race not sinning, and dwelling in the garden of Eden ; and remember that the garden of Eden appears but twice in Scripture as the alpha and omega of its scenery. Such a race would have a Tree of life in their reach from which they could constantly eat; and, by some process of elimination, sudden or gradual, they would cleanse out of them the mortal parts, expel the flesh and blood which cannot now, and probably as much then, could not inherit the kingdom of God. In such a case an individual would not fear hell, not having sinned; but he would need this fruit, in order to live forever (see *Gen.* iii. 22). The clay in which he was moulded must be cast out, and a spiritual body take its place.

This story, we use here, *only* as an illus-

tration. We say *only*, from want of
space. Now, that we have sinned and
have to expel *the phronema sarkos*, as well
as the clay; the pitch of sin, as well as the
animal nature; the process, which is to
work out salvation for 'body, soul and
spirit,' must include all helps which
would have been necessary to a sinless
race, and more. There must then be a
divine sense, in which Christ offers to us,
after a spiritual and heavenly manner,
His very body and blood. The work to
be done takes in *our bodies* as well as our
souls. Jesus meant to be understood as
reaching both, when He said, "Except ye
eat the flesh of the Son of Man and
drink His blood, ye have no life in
you;" and again: "The words that I
speak unto you, they are Spirit and they
are life." Possibly we do not *understand*
all this: possibly we may accept it, as the
sayings of One *who did.* Our sinful bodies
are to be made clean by His body; our
souls washed through His blood, that

we may evermore dwell in Him and He in us. How may these things be? This was the question of Nicodemus; and the answer then was, and must be now, 'The wind bloweth' in mystic circles, and its sound was heard—its laws then unknown. So there is a limit of mortal knowledge. We accept the known and yearn after the celestial, until God's time shall come. But our intelligent faith in an intercommunion between Christ and ourselves, joins us to Him in body, soul and spirit, and we die in Him calmly, knowing that in Him we also rise again. We hear a man like John Calvin saying, after certain absurdities of transubstantiation are rejected by him: "I willingly admit anything which helps to express the true and substantial communication of the body and blood of the Lord, as exhibited to believers under the sacred symbols of the Lord's Supper, understanding that they are received *not by the imagination or* *intellect merely*, but are enjoyed *in reality as the food of eternal life.*"*

Two subjects crowd on us on the Thursday of the command : 1. The Viaticum † which Jesus received. 2. The Prayer, in which His soul took conscious leave of common life.

I. The relation of the Lord's Supper to death. We pass all questions of dispute, and keep to the single point, first, as to His own passion, and next to our individual sense of coming departure. The two great laws of the generation (birth) and conservation (food) of the natural body, interpret to us the mysteries of God's work in the soul by divine appointment. *Born-again*—tells of the beginning of the spirit of life in the soul,

---

* *Institutes*, Bk. iv. chap. xvii. 219.

† We may use a word which Bishop Burnet had no scruple at : "He received the sacrament on his knees, with great devotion, which it may be supposed was the greater, because he apprehended it to be the last, and so took it as his *viaticum* and provision for his journey."— *Life of Sir W. Hale.*

and then, by consequence, of the spiritual body. The life immortal and perfect was first hidden in a tree in the Garden of Eden. The Israelites, as all others, '*partook* of the sacrifice,' and held a religious sense as always contained in the true actual partakers of the table, either of the Lord or of devils (*i.e.* idols). The true spiritual covenant in the Gospel does not and cannot afford to neglect this common faith of mankind. By all the language taken from the "similitudes of things seen in the Mount" of God by Moses, there must have been in the Gospel this unity of belief. It is the link between us and all past systems of religion, not as a bald teaching, but as a vital centre. Whether our Lord Himself partook of the bread and wine, at this Supper, and for what ends, it were impertinent for us to discuss. He celebrated it, after a *longing* which had eagerly anticipated it. "With desire have I desired to eat this passover with

you *before I suffer."—St. Mark* xiv. 17.
Surely in that desire to eat with them, the
new passover had been included. He
was not without a keen wish to go through
this scene of God's ancient love with
them, and no less of God's future mercy
to them, in a past passover and in the one
to come. As a mysterious Being, He
stooped to us. It is with Him, as man,
that we have to do, in looking to trace
His steps, which we desire to follow;
and only such steps as we can follow,
when our time at last shall come.

Jesus, as an obedient Israelite, by this
"sign upon His hand and this memorial
between His eyes," consciously fulfilled
all righteousness, and, in so doing, found
that scriptural words, unlike all others,
are *alive*, and spring up out of the past
into His own present. As Man, there
was in Him the workings of faith and the
exercise of graces, which we need, and
for which need we look to Him for example and help. Of faith it is often sung,

"Events long past it can renew
And long foresee the things to come."

No faith is so strong and natural as that which has a visible object, on which to fasten in this effort to recall the past or forecast the future. God has rarely left any man with merely abstract words about Himself, but adds some visible sign as the intermediary between us and the invisible world. We are body and soul commingled. God in mercy joins faith to deeds and to visible ordinances; to dramatic symbols or personal experiences, by which we fasten on the visible and so reach upward to the invisible. Jesus would look through the lenses of this ancient feast which had been adjusted in the covenants of the past to the mystical top of Horeb, and see the heavenly similitudes before He leaves the world for them.

One cause of the reluctance of Christians to entertain the frequent and comfortable consideration of this great event of their lives, namely its short passage to another world, is their lack of faith in that *Communion of saints*, which sustained our Lord at this time. This is the evil of our sectarian disputes. Whether the Holy Church be any one, defined organism, or a company of all faithful people under all varieties of polity, from Fenelon to Fox, we alike do not easily love, what we are forced all the while to dispute about. The father leaving home for a campaign to fight for his and other like homes, is full of zeal for the object of his warm recollections: the common trooper, whose life is spent in the saddle and in skirmishings without number, is usually found to battle by habit, and with no special stirring of his passionate zeal for quiet home-joys. So we may fancy a Christian armed and prepared by a great practical Churchly life, to feel himself so entirely one of a company of 'pilgrims and strangers,' as to lose individual fear and gloom in his other consciousness, as one in Christ Jesus with all the saints.

The theory of the Church of Christ seems to have fixed itself in the mind of St. Paul, as he advanced on his course out of Judaism, in a confirmed faith in its universality, as one living, organic whole. We may say of him, that his theory of it (to use common language of to-day) was like that of astronomers now, concerning the solar system. They tell us of vast spaces filled with fire-mist or nebulous matter circling inward at the word of God, and fed by all the comets and visitants of space, drawn in toward a common centre, and feeding as they come, either the sun himself, or drawn to any planet passing near, ministering to it as it circles in its predestined order around the source of light.

A Judaic school would have had the Church beginning from Jerusalem and circling by centrifugal force outward; but the Apostle to the Gentiles reached the true solution of a centripetal law

—all flowing inward to "One Lord, one faith, one baptism, one God and Father of all."* The Epistle to Ephesus contains the doctrine of "one Holy Catholic Church." To realize in practical heart-beats, what it means to each one of us, is a work which would reward us for any labor or trial. Partial results are seen to overcome the evil of false doctrine and grievous errors on other points. We would reason thus: we are made members of a mystical body, in which we are thenceforth particles borne in the blood of that body, carried by it to results past our individual knowledge; used for purposes only dimly comprehended by us; and if faithful, entering into its organic life and doing a work in accomplishing the will of God, infinite

---

* It may be noted, by the way, that our Lord gave the twelve their commission *beginning at Jerusalem;* and gave St. Paul his mission, ending at Jerusalem. Two transverse-currents are required on the electric circle: and why not two, on that which brings us news from the Father of lights?

in goodness, beauty and glory.   Fancy a
minute globule of blood in the artery ; so
small that only the strong microscope
can show it to the eye.   Fancy it to be
endued with thought and will : and then
give it our vanity, pride and folly ; and
what a satire does it read us.   Or take as
an illustration the minute coral insect,
under the vast superincumbent mass of
ocean ; toiling in its little cell to do its
functional work.   What may it know of
the immense shudderings of ocean—of
the currents rolling to both poles—of the
storm-winds that agitate the upper deep,
of monsters that rush by it, and send
against it an eddy, a millionth part of
which suffices to crush a myriad of such
little mites.   But God is with it, and
His Law holds it in its place ; and in His
mighty purposes, it is counted and never
forgotten.   It does its little mason-work
and dies out.   Ages roll away, and an
atol or an island rears its front on such
foundations : and man lives there and

yearns toward the infinite, not unaided by his little, brother-insect.

Thus are we to the love of Christ, whose height, depth, length and breadth are ocean-like and past finding out; each one building his cell, and filling out his day; and all the while a greater Will and Purpose, which uses ages as a second and accepts our little deed, prepares an *ideal*, which shall be worthy to be the Bride of the "God of God and Light of Light;" in which we can be particles of light, shining as the stars forever and ever, surging with joy, burning with love and ever renewing splendor and glory as we shine. We call the deed of this day—*the communion*—the fellowship, the symbol and living recognition of the polity and present body of that Church. Now, simply, as a habit of mind; if one goes into the Dark, intensely self-conscious, self-bounded, self-reliant —death is only an unmitigated evil, to be abhorred, hated, dreaded and put away. If, on the other hand, as a habit of mind, he goes about daily, working for all, finding Christ in all, and bringing before him in all his deeds and prayers, studies and thoughts, that he is one of a communion of saints; one of a life that never ends—feeling himself to be one in a body, whose Head is already in heaven; he learns to go through the vale of life, as Elijah across the desert, sustained by angel's food, to the cave where he meets God, to hear from Him that there are thousands who bow not the knee to Baal. It is this habit of Church-consciousness that makes the Holy Supper to be angels' food to our faith. Jesus in that Passover began the great sacrament of the Communion of saints, and saw in spirit the *travail of His soul*, and was satisfied.

II. For our sakes that feast was to be incorporated into His great human consciousness, and take its part in the work of atonement and reconciliation. No one

is strong, who only dreams of food.   No
faith is vigorous in wholesome endurance
which despises the law of increment in
visible ordinances.   Take the highest
dream known to us mortals.   Fancy
that one, by pure spiritual up-rousing of
the mind, soul, and spirit, can fly up beyond Uranus and Sirius and out beyond
the sweet influences of the Pleiades, beyond that star *Alcyone* of present signi-
ficant study, and have no stop in the
vast immense, until the dim star dust shall
be as far behind him, as it is now before ; there to find *the throne of God Pan-
tocrator*, and be saved by his own activity
and intrinsic yearnings of faith.   What
then ? We believe that Jesus in this
passover found help and strength as He
looked back on Adam's sin and fall, and
'Abraham's day,' on Moses' call at the
burning-bush, on Israel's night of full
moon on the great 14th Nisan in Egypt,
and heard the dreary shriek of Egyptians,
and the roar of the Red Sea as it destroyed

their armies. In a word that He had a faith
as *man,* in all perfection, unapproacha-
ble by us, but yet that He "with desire
desired" to eat that passover. True, it
was in all love for us, but could that love
help us, if He did not yearn for it and
need it as one of us? as with us having
the natural fear of death? If He was
perfect man, that is a man "tried in all
points like as we are, the reply must be
in the affirmative. So then a practical
rule comes in, that we find *that faith* as
He found it: not among the stars so
much as in the way of obedience; and
that we prepare us for the Lord's Supper,* .
and go back over the past, as it were with
the elements in our hands, as the alpha-
betic signs of the heavenly language; and
"in His bleeding love displayed" find
the stimulus to a vigorous and educated
faith. Bishop Jeremy Taylor has well

---

* There is no little debate as to the propriety of the
celebration of the Lord's Supper after dark. We refer the
curious to *Bingham's Antiq., Book* xxi. § 30.

said, that a man should be as careful to
prepare for the Lord's Supper as he would
prepare for death, and for like reasons.
Does not a greater than he appear to us,
as joining for us the two extremes of
thought, a soul and body saved in His
covenant? and the way to that consciousness which we call *hope*, by the means of
the Paschal celebration? However much
one may intensify the activity of faith in
what is *present* at the time, he reaps not
all the advantage of it, unless he can
reach out to the past and future, and
learn for himself how this Supper was related in the mind of Jesus, to His dying,
and how to ours. "Ye do show the
Lord's death." He that eateth, not dis-
cerning the Lord's body, eats condemnation (krisin). He is to examine himself, and so eat ; and if he do not try to
prepare himself, he is obnoxious to the
warning. "For this cause many are
weak and sickly among you and many
sleep." We claim merely this much,

avoiding debate, that there was in such a consciousness as this language indicates, a thought of the union of this great feast of *faith* and man's vital life, not as a physical cause to him of sickness or health, but a vital dynamic, taking in his whole being, which has all been re-deemed with the blood of Christ.

We confine the remark to our one point, that as it did with Christ, it now mingles in with our life; and especially with our death. That faith is best, which can find, as its own 'hour of darkness' draws on, that in it there is a *longing* for this provision by the way, a deep, unut-terable harmony in the visible and invis-ible, so that it would fain think of the old 14th Nisan, as the moon looked down on a dark angel of death retreating southwards, and a nation of redeemed ones, turning their faces toward the east in flight : and no less recall the other full moon of Nisan, when, under the olives of

Gethsemane, its own way to eternal life was manifested.

II. The sublime prayer of Jesus is our spiritual viaticum as well. "Father, my work is done. Take me, take them whom I have loved with me, that we all may be one." The sting of death is sin. But many a man believes strongly, perhaps very roughly, but believes firmly, that sin is pardoned. For all that believing, death glooms on him from his bed-head, as a foul and evil harpy, which touches and soils all things. The pang of nature which is left unsoothed is its *fearful partings, its dreadful, unrelieved loneliness.* Our natural affections are wrenched apart and we go off alone. *'I shall die alone,'* said Paschal. Jesus died fearfully alone, and deserted of all. His last act before He went to meet it, was by prayer to bring His own lonely consciousness in the 'innumerable company of the elect'—to offer Himself in prayer— as He was also to offer Himself in blood

—for all the saints; to look out of Himself to them, to call them all before Him,
'the hundred and forty and four thousand' of Israel's sons : and beyond them
the countless multitudes, like "the dew of
the morning." He saw the travail of His
soul and was satisfied. He drank of the
brook by the way; therefore shall He
lift up His head. Does any one of us take
home the moral? A soldier is struck by
a bullet, just as his heart swells with
victory, that his country and its numberless homes are safe, and goes into Paradise without a pang. A Christian believer wrings his hands, as the last hour
draws near, because of its *partings.* Is
there not 'balm in Gilead' for this
sorrow? We see Jesus, who loved His
own to the end, loved them as tenderly
as any father : loved them as weakly and
tearfully as pure natures always love—
foreseeing this pang as *before Him* and
us, taking them all up in His arms, and
holding death at bay—as He lays them

at the feet of the Omnipotent, and in the sublime of self-abnegation, passes before us ; if not yet, as 'more than conqueror,' certainly not less, over that fear which holds us all in bondage. Try it, reader, and so yearn for the heavenly food, which gives us this unearthly life—that we may, on these 14th Nisans, and on that which is so fast coming on, that sometimes we seem to hear the weeks and days fly like a weaver's shuttle—so fast they click by—that we may eat the Saviour's precious food, and pray His holy prayer, and cease to fear.

Almighty and Everliving God, we most heartily thank Thee, for that Thou dost vouchsafe to feed us with holy mysteries ; assist us with Thy grace to continue in the holy fellowship of Thy Church and to do all such good works as thou hast prepared for us to walk in, through Jesus Christ our Lord. *Amen.*

Good Friday.

March 26.   True Era A.D. *28.*

" Lo I come *to do Thy will*, O God. * * * By the which
will we are sanctified through the offering of the body
of Jesus Christ once for all."—*Heb.* ix. 9, 10.

" Is it not strange, the darkest hour
   That ever dawn'ed on sinful earth
   Should touch the heart with softer powei
   For comfort, than an angel's mirth ?
   That to the Cross the mourner's eye should turn,
   Sooner than when the stars of Christmas burn ?"

THE two days here run into one.
    With us Thursday ends at mid-
night : with the Jews, Friday had already
begun, when the sun was setting.   There
is no pause to break the interval.   The
disciples stupidly sleep, when watching
might have kindled some sense in them,
of the events to come.   Their disciple-

ship has really ended : they are about to
flee at the first shock of evil ; and all,
because, they did not look beyond that
cherished dream of a kingdom of this
world.   So is it with us : and we trace
these Lenten scenes over and over in
vain, if we do not learn to look through
them into the life of things.   In the
early evening they have passed out of
the city and are in the solitude of the
Kedron valley.   A few olive trees partly
shade them from the light of the full
moon.   Possibly the Kedron, which was
a winter stream, may have tinkled feebly
along its rocky bed.   The disciples weary
now, slumber while Jesus bows in agony
of prayer, and the great act begins which
abolishes the older covenant and estab-
lishes the new—in faith of which, winning
us to follow Him, we are made holy to
God, and the Spirit of Christ is given to
us ; and divine life arises in the soul, and
beats and waves of spiritual light reach
it, which bind it never to rest again, till

it finds that ethereal light, even at the foot of the Golden Throne.

Gethsemane is to Calvary what intention is to the execution, or the will to the doing. The wrecker on a wild, storm-beaten shore of crags looks out and sees the flash of the gun which tells him that his fellow-men are in trouble. He pauses and shivers as the louder blast howls defiance at his rising intention. But he hears an echo from Calvary that teaches him to act, no matter at what peril. A voice of God is calling him to save them, and in his rude way, he puts forth the life-boat and toils and battles through the storm on his errand of mercy, in imitation of Christ. So the same voice is in all true life. We see Jesus in the garden, and solemn awe gathers over us, as we behold Him look out to the coming storm, in which the powers of darkness have their hour. He bows His sacred head in confession that it is dreadful and terrifying, even as great waves of trouble and horror.   He is ready for a sad *De profundis*.   Reader, every quake and tremor of nature are acknowledged in that thrice repeated prayer.   "Father, it it be possible, let this cup pass from Me !"

Shall we say that He was *deserted* by God, or that His pure humanity is daunted at the leaden thunder clouds before him !   If He must have been *deserted* in order to suffer thus, then we too may look to see our dying beds deserted, and our faith confessedly weakest where it ought to be strongest.   If on the other hand His human soul went down as Job into 'the belly of hell;' or as Schiller's pearl diver, into the very depths of the dreadful maelstrom, and confessed the pangs and throes of that agony for our sakes ; we need not fear to follow Him, nor mourn and murmur that God is far from us, and has forgotten to be gracious, at the very time when His hand is on us "mighty to save," and the new life is just beginning.

It is not for faith to say that Christ died for us, until it can feel that His spirit and mind are being made over to us. There must be points where the real in Him becomes an actual power in us. Beyond the fact of His death lies the law of it—what it teaches us and what it becomes in us. The Jew of Solomon's day kneeled before the great porch of the temple. Faith taught him that behind the vail was the mercy seat, where between the cherubim of the golden cover of the ark was the mystic centre and vital life of his covenant and nation, even the presence of God. But, as God looked out from thence at him kneeling, the sacred scrutiny was directed not altogether to his faith in the unseen, but to his consciousness, how that faith was moulding him, and what sort of man it was all the while making him. We sometimes lose the vital core of the faith, in the effort to grasp and systematize and defend the dogmas of Catholic thought

concerning the ineffable and mysterious
nature of the *unseen* in Christ ; His mystical Sonship, His singleness of Person,
reaching out into two natures; His ' love
past finding out,' in pouring out His
heart's blood tinged with the light and
sympathy of the Infinite—and we sometimes possibly forget, that while sinful
man may often presume and intrude in
sacred things, he may also as often fail
by stupidness ; and hope to be saved by
superstitious and miraculous dreams where
God saves him by truth.   He who would
find Jesus on the passage along the dark
valley and *via dolorosa*—to make himself
His true follower, has need of all help ;
and as he confesses that the cup which
Christ drank is a wonder of agony and
atoning love, he himself must compass
in some way to find his way to it, by
something more than either dogmatical
correctness of opinion, or sentimental
offers of fancied sympathy.   We say that
he needs all helps.   Yea, all are not too

many for us. The human soul that reaches the electric-shock of the mystic power hid in the dying of this Lamb of God must neglect no means that God has given him to use.

We offer first a few words, on the clue to the historic events of the day.

After the betrayal of Jesus, the crowd go first to the house of Annas. He was the strongest man as to state-craft and energy of all his race. When we remember the 'mighty deeds,' which they knew were told of Christ, it was a dangerous lion they were playing with. It was by no means strange, that they go first to the ruling mind of all, with their prisoner. Thence they go, probably no great distance, to the house of Caiphas the high-priest in office, where the governing senate of the nation, the Sanhedrim, was in session. The tumult and disorder is plainly that of men who are very anxious and fearful, lest this prophet of Galilee may call down some

of that legion of angels to confound them.
Strangely enough after curious worry and
excitement their charge finally settles on
that one accusation against Him, which
was true in words, which they knew to
be true, as He said it, and afterwards
betray such knowledge : that charge
which rings out to us the truth under
all the scene : "This One said, destroy
this temple, and in three days I will raise
it up." They pretend disloyalty in Him
to the material temple. They go the
next day to Pilate to show their false-
ness, confessing that they understood
His meaning, all the time,* of a spiritual
building.

Thence about daylight (it is near the
vernal equinox and the Jewish hours are
at this season like our own) they go to
the Castle of Antonia to Pilate. He sends
Jesus to Herod, and on His return gives
sentence against Him. About the hour
of the Morning Sacrifice, nine o'clock as

---

* *Matt.* xxvii. 63.

we reckon, He was crucified, and at the hour of Evening Sacrifice, three in the afternoon, He yields up His soul to God.

As the Sabbath, which was a "highday," is hastening on, they hurry their wretched work, and ask that the bodies may be put away : and as the setting-sun again shines its last on a world redeemed forever by their deed, the work of atoning love is done, and our minds forget them, to go down to the world of spirits* whither Jesus went, to ponder what is there. The pale form of the Son of Man sleeps in the cave of the rich man of Arimathea,† and John and perhaps Peter with him, and the Virgin Mother, mourn in hopeless despair. The warning of the aged Simeon had been accomplished. " Yea, a sword shall pierce through thine own soul also."‡ The Shepherd had

---

* " He descended into Hell."—*Apostles' Creed.*

† The legend is that Joseph was imprisoned for this, by the Jews.

‡ *Luke* ii. 35.

been smitten and the sheep were scattered.
Darkness hung over Bethany on this
night, and great searchings of heart were
experienced by all those who had trusted
that "it had been He who should have
redeemed Israel." •And if indeed there
be no resurrection, and if really Christ
has not risen from that tomb, then they
and we and all men are yet in their sins,
and they who are fallen asleep are all
perished. It is therefore to us all, the
most solemn spot of earth ; the critical
point of all thought and meditation as
Christians.   We aim in this brief re-
view only to point out such sources of
devout consideration as may be suitable
to our simple design, which, be it remembered, is to make the death of Christ the
model of our own.

   1. Christ was "very God and very
man ; who truly suffered, was crucified,
dead and buried to reconcile His Father
to us and to be a sacrifice, not only for
original guilt, but also for actual sins of

men."* He suffered "death on the
cross for our redemption ; who made there
(by His one oblation of Himself, once
offered) a full, perfect and sufficient sacrifice, oblation and satisfaction for the
sins of the whole world."† In words
like these the Church confesses the mystery of the atonement, and cuts off all
false and heretical teaching. It is a mystery, and may not be put in words any
farther than it has been done, by the
mould-thoughts of the ancient, inspired
Scriptures. They who dare not come up
to those forms are timid, to their own
loss. They who go beyond them are
rash, to their own injury. *Sacrifice, oblation, satisfaction,* were all moulded by
God's own order of Providence. Ages
rolled by as He was giving them a meaning in the religious life of Israel, never to
be lost. *Redemption* was struck out at a
white heat, when God *bought off* His

---

* Second of the Thirty-nine Articles of Religion.
† The Order for the Holy Communion.

elect people out of the fiery furnace ot
Egyptian bondage, with a bloody rite.
Priest, altar, reconciliation, atonement, all
take their roots in the entire history of
man ; and in Christ speak better things
than the blood of Abel.   That spake of
God's acceptance strongly enough, since .
it was the cause of his premature departure.   God accepted him, but took him
away from earth.   God accepted Christ,
and sent Him back to tell us of the love
of God.

All these sacred words tell of a mystery
which is an object of faith.   It confounds
reason.   It says to science, "Thus far
and no farther, and here shall thy proud
waves be stayed."   We can only bow and
adore the love 'that passeth knowledge ;'
whose height and depth and length and
breadth, are like God, past finding out.
The truth has one proof to us, which we
can feel.   Those who accept these terms
in their fulness are seen in all ages to
cling closely to the Scriptures, old and

new; and to combine in solid, regular religious life about them; and one by one to
die quietly in the comfort of a "reason-
able, religious and holy hope," while the
rest of men, like the wild tribes around
the Israelites in the wilderness, vary and
wander and disappear. We kneel before
the temple vail which is rent now for us :
but rent as the mystic sacrifice was com-
pleted, which proclaimed God reconciled
to us. This faith in "thoughts that are
higher than our thoughts," and ways that,
in mercy and love, are not as our ways,
is the wholesome centre of our Christian
life. "Behold the Lamb of God that
taketh away the sin of the world," said
the first St. John, to simple provincials ;
and their deeper life began to run its
course. On the throne of glory, surround-
ed by the four Cherubim and the twice
twelve elders, receiving the hallelujahs of
all created beings, the other John saw
"A Lamb as it had been slain," opening the book of all mystery and reveal-

ing to earth the perfected will of God.

> " Born for this He meets His Passion,
>   Gives Himself an offering free :
> On the cross the Lamb is lifted,
>   There a sacrifice to be."

Sorrows were there too deep for human tongue. Clouds hung over the cold stone * of Golgotha, while that love was perfected, by which we are sanctified.

But we may claim to seize each help that is at hand, and climb by it up to the foot of the Cross, and kindle our love for this holy Saviour.

Christ died *for us*, for you, for me. We have part in His death. Other mysteries stun and confuse men with blind faith, and leave them torpid ; this one is pregnant with the power of an endless life. Even as we feel that the heart which is broken over us is of infinite resource ; it is also a man's heart, which asks our

---

* It is perhaps well to banish the idea of a *mountain*, for which there is no authority, and see instead the lonely rock, which, from its general shape, was called *Calvarion 'ull.*

sympathy and love, and interprets to us the lessons of divine help.

Christ died in sorrow beyond any that we can ever have. To human eyes His life was a failure. He had been building up a system, that crumbled at a touch. His very friends fled ignominiously from His side. All that He had done had been strangely transient and unreal. He had healed men, taught them, helped them, but where were they now? Doubtless the exultation of Caiphas was almost *divine* in his own estimation, as he taunted Him, "He saved others, Himself He cannot save." A world's masculine judgment was recorded against Him as the sun went down. Only a few women, one young man and a dying malefactor, were there to wonder at Him and weep. For the moment put thyself in His place, and think of His past, as the weary eyes sank heavily; and the dry throat cried out its "*Eloi! Eloi! lama sabacthani?*" over a life ending in such a day. Then take

to thine heart the lesson, that no sorrow,
save sin, can separate thee from that love

We will few of us share His physical
agony ; for many a Christian has been
translated into Paradise on the instant,
and without pain. But for us He ful-
filled the largest type of sorrow, and
drank a cup which superhuman skill
had mingled with wormwood and gall,
that we might accept our diluted portions.
" If we suffer with Him, we shall reign
with Him."   Drop out all notion of
charms in religion, and substitute *truth*
and *reality* for them.   Then do one thing
more.   Look to the spirit more than to
the letter, and escape the monkish
notion, that only certain voluntary acts
ensure this reward and oneness of
sorrow.   Look on all the trials of a
Christian's life as empurpled with the
blood of the covenant-seal, and take
them all to Christ.   Many Christians err,
by putting their religion in a few specific
acts and experiences.   They would say,

'a missionary dying in a heathen land has this right of oneness with Christ;' but we claim that a man in his family, that any one in any relation or condition, believing in Christ, in any true sorrow rightly borne, has this oneness of sympathy. So all of us may claim it, in the thought of death. I am to die, to find some 'place of a skull,' where the carnal joy ceases, and flesh and heart fail; where clouds cover the sun and the solid earth quakes; where a trembling flesh and racked nerves pull down the defences of the citadel of life, and the heavy surge of a *De profundis* dashes afar on the briny shores of a dark, boundless sea. Must I then be eager to die dramatically, in one scenic method, so as then to find Christ my friend? No! I may now so draw near to Him in love, so regulate the beat of my heart to His, so learn of Him the lessons of His teaching, that then the sinking heart will keep its habitual action.

"In grief and fear I drank, alas
 The bitter cup that would not pass ;
   Then like my Lord I knelt and prayed,
 And in mine own Gethsemane
 I found the One Who died for me."

Dear Bishop Gadsden went out of life so slowly, that all his faculties failed him one after another, and we could almost see him, as a pilgrim, lay them down one by one, as he passed the stations on that sad road. But the last to fail him was the habit of saying the Lord's Prayer, which he had learned at his mother's knee, and that went with him to the end : so that the prayer which he began here, he ended with a start, where saints and angels chanted to him the Amen. There is a law of " reflex action " in the soul, as well as in the body. These sacred seasons of Holy Church, when wisely used, year by year, until the *cross* gathers all one's heart to it, establish a pulse in it, which identifies it with Christ and makes it His by a fixed law.

God gave His only begotten Son to die for us. In other words, He gave us

His dearest thing to win us, to give Him
our all in return.   This is the great con-
tract of the cross.   Abraham was to stab
his 'only-begotten son, his dearest, the
pride of his old age;' and then watch him
die; and then burn him to ashes for God.
And as the old man, with uplifted hand
to obey the dire command, was stopped,
and saw what it all meant that he should
have been so tortured; he "saw the
day of Christ and was glad;" he caught
the ideal under the Cross.   He leads us
to it as a princely Father of the faithful,
that we may learn to give all to God; and
listen to that sublime song of the Lamb,
until we are in harmony with it.   To
so believe, by oft reiteration, in Christ and
what Christ did, as the one true thing,
and the only thing to do, the safest,
wisest and best, that we can mortify
the deeds of the body, and so crucify the
evil lusts of carnal life, as to come to the
last scene of all, pure and clean in the
marriage garment of the King, and walk

willingly to our rest in Him, is the problem of the Christian life. O Saviour of the world, who by Thy Cross and precious blood hast redeemed us, save us and help us, we beseech Thee, O Lord!

Easter Even.

March 27.   True Era, A.D. *28.*

"They said, therefore, What is this that He saith, *a
little while ?*   We cannot tell what He saith."—*St. John*
xvi. 18.

" What then ? I am not careful to inquire ;
 I know there will be tears, and fears, and sorrow ;
And then a loving Saviour drawing nigher,
 And saying, ' *I* will answer for the morrow.'

" What then ? a shadowy valley, lone and dim ;
 And then, a deep and darkly rolling river ;
And then a flood of light, a seraph's hymn,
 And God's own smile forever and forever !"

                                    JANE CREWSON.

THE first activity around the silent
tomb of Jesus, was that of fiercest
hatred.   The Pharisees confess that they
had understood the saying of Jesus, as
to the temple of His body; and beg of
Pilate that the tomb may be secured.

They go there and seal it: first undoubtedly satisfying themselves that the body was still within. This would be after sunset and before dark on Saturday. After sunset ; as the Sabbath ended then, and they, forsooth ! were scrupulous men : and before it was too dark to identify the circumstances. We suppose that Joseph and Nicodemus had hastily deposited the body of Jesus on Friday evening, perhaps a little before sunset, and that the Marys watched the place until dark, and returned to the city. As to the eleven disciples, did ever men so utterly fail—John excepted—and desert a Leader for whom they had volunteered allegiance only a few hours previously ! No man seems to have marked or watched the spot. The Pharisees, if they had known it, need not have feared, lest any disciples should have 'come by night and stolen Him away.' They had lost faith and heart. They have no bond to hold them together any longer, and seem to linger around Jerusalem with no special design or object in life.

The hours passed without any other incident than this sealing of the tomb, from Friday evening until the earthquake on Sunday morning, before day.

We turn to the other side of the tomb ; which, though yet mostly unrevealed to us, has in it certain rays and lines of light, which are very precious. Possibly the best and most connected view of the whole subject of the Descent into the Under-world, is that which is contained in the apocryphal work of the second century, called *The Gospel of Nicodemus.* We offer it, much as we should suggest to a stranger the Pilgrim's Progress of Bunyan as a general view of the practical Christian doctrine of the seventeenth and eighteenth centuries. We fancy that the portion of this Gospel of Nicodemus which relates the descent into Hades, was somewhat of a similar work, a vision changed to a history, to declare what was thought of it by the early Christians. Of course, whether the frame-work was at first fanciful or not, the simple people of that age would soon come to regard it as solid history. It may be questioned whether we have improved on the story, or increased our store of consolation in times of affliction, now that centuries have passed.

Tischendorf attributes this work to the second century, which is probably too early ; though without doubt *the legend was formed by the end of the second century.* * This fact is quite enough for our purpose, which is to reproduce this ancient vision of Christ's descent into Hell. One may prudently gather up all the Scriptural texts, and see how closely they agree with it ; yea, sometimes more than they do with our jejune, and, if not semi-skeptical, certainly *our unimaginative* orthodoxy. We use, for brevity's sake,

---

* See Ante-Nicene Library, Apoch. Gos., etc., *Preface.*

the translation of the Latin version, which may have been the original, for all we know. We offer only the outline of the story.

Three Rabbis, who had come up from Galilee, rose up in the Sanhedrim, when it was in utter perplexity about the rumors which were rife in Jerusalem after the resurrection, and stated that they had met at the Jordan a multitude of the fathers of Israel who had been *a long time dead ;* and especially, that they had identified two of the number, *Karinus* and *Leucius,* very dear friends, whom they had known to have been dead, and had seen buried in their graves. From them they learned . that Christ had "raised them from the lower world ; * that the gates and bars of the *Under-world* (Hades) had been destroyed, the souls of saints

---

* "And the graves were opened, and many bodies of the saints which slept, arose, and came out of the graves *after His resurrection,* and went into the holy city and appeared unto many."—*St. Matt.* xxvii. 52, 53.

taken out of it and exalted *with* Christ to
a supernal sphere. They were walking
for a time around Judea, not speaking
to all persons, nor indeed to any, without the divine permission. Nor would
they have addressed those Rabbis, unless
it had been allowed them by the Holy
Spirit.

Annas and Caiaphas suggested the
simple test of first discovering whether
the bodies of these two men could be
found, and the assembly agreed to the
proposition. Fifteen men, ' fit for the
duty,' who knew where they had died
and where they had been buried, went
at once to the spot where they had seen
them laid, and found the tomb opened,
and "very many others besides, and
found neither a sign of their bones nor
their dust." They returned in haste, and
reported to the assembly. The Sanhedrim was in grief and perplexity. They
next send out Nicodemus, Joseph and
the three Rabbis of Galilee, who go wan-

dering about the valley of the Jordan and the neighboring hills.

'Behold suddenly from Mount Amalech, as it were twelve thousand men appear, singing an Easter chant.' They are terrified and fall to the ground; but hear a message, that they shall find the two men sought for, in their own houses. This they do, and convoy them to the presence of the great assembly in Jerusalem. On solemn adjuration by the priests to tell them the truth, Karinus and Leucius make signs for pen and paper, and go apart into separate cells to write out their statements. They finish together, and together say Amen. Karinus gave his paper to Annas, and Leucius, his to Caiaphas, "and saluting each other, they went out, and returned to their sepulchres."

The two accounts agree miraculously letter to letter, and are read before the assembly, to this effect:

Karinus and Leucius were in the

lower world, in darkness * and the shadow
of death, and suddenly a great light or
luminousness shone, and Hades † and
the gates of Death trembled. A voice
known as that of the Son of God, as a great
thunder afar off, is heard saying : "Lift
up your gates, ye princes ; Lift up the
everlasting gates and the king of Glory,
Christ the Lord, shall enter in."

Satan came fleeing in terror, and commanded to shut and bolt all the gates,
and make ready for war. Hideous howl-
ings and din ensues. Satan orders
Hades, "Make thyself ready for Him, I
shall bring Him down to thee." Hades

---

* "Before I go, whence I shall not return," said Job,
"to the land of darkness and the shadow of death, a land
of darkness, as darkness itself, without any order, and
where the light is as darkness."—*Job* x. 21, 22 ; *Isa.* xiv.
9–12.

† Hades is a *person*—as he is in the vision of Isaiah and
of St. John (*Isa.* xiv. 9 ; *Rev.* vi. 8 ; xx. 13, 14. Compare
1 *Cor.* xv. 55), of which Milton has caught the idea,
though he makes him a female :

> "the snaky sorceress that sat
> Fast by hell gate, and kept the fatal key."
> *Par. Lost*, Book ii. 723.

replies, "The voice heard was the voice of the Son of the Most High—myself and my dungeons are all open ; bring Him not to me, or we are lost." Satan recapitulates the scenes of the cross, how Jesus had died, impotent to save Himself.

Then Hades said to him : "If he be the same who, by the mere command, 'Lazarus, come forth' (*St. John* xi. 43), made Lazarus fly like an eagle from my bosom, when he had been dead four days, he is not a man in humanity, but God in majesty. I entreat thee bring him not to me." Satan persists, and wrangles with the other.

The saints hear and are at first stunned by noises in the land of silence ; not yet recognizing each other, though in the possession of all their faculties. Adam addresses Satan, to warn him of his coming fate. A curious scene succeeds between Adam and his posterity, and Seth relates the old myth of his journey after the "oil of compassion" for his dying father. Isaiah takes up the tale, and the hermit spirit of John the Baptist follows. He relates how a voice from heaven had adopted Jesus as His beloved Son. Adam and David and Jeremy are introduced on the scene, beginning the ceaseless Alleluia : when again comes the Voice nearer, as of a great thunder : " Lift up your gates, ye princes, and be ye lifted up, ye everlasting doors, and the king of glory will come in." Satan and Hades respond, "Who is the king of glory ?" and it was answered to them by the Voice : "The Lord, strong and mighty, the Lord, mighty in battle."

Just then comes a spirit of a robber carrying a cross on his shoulders, crying on the outside, "Open, that I may come in." Satan opens the door a little, and takes him in. The saints ask an explanation of his cross, and learn his story ; and that Jesus is following him.

Again the old Hebrew chant is begun

by the Voice without, and the bars and gates of Hell break up and fly asunder. Jesus appears, travelling in light : Satan is bound and cast down into Tartarus, under the guardianship of Hades, who plunges with him into the lake of fire, into the depth of the abyss.

The Lord receives His servants, and they crowd about Him, singing that new song of redemption, till now unheard. Jesus set His cross in the midst of Hades —"the sign of victory, and which will remain even to eternity."

Then all went thence along with the Lord, leaving Satan and Hades in Tartarus, or the bottomless pit. To many of us, says Karinus, "it was commanded that we should rise in the body, giving the world a testimony of the resurrection of the Lord Jesus Christ, and of those things which had been done in the lower world."

When this paper was read to the Jews, a great weeping was heard : "Woe to us! we have shed sacred blood upon the earth!"

They lamented forty days and forty nights their guilty deed—and the Lord 'pitiful, affectionate, and most high,' did not then destroy them. Thus ends the testimonies of Karinus and Leucius.

It is doubtless easy to find weak points in this ancient writing—and to fault the scenery of it. We hesitate not to aver, that it is far more easy to reconcile it with the language of the entire Scriptures in all its main points.

There is not a word about *purgatory*,* or indulgences and pardons in it. The fond conceits of later ages sprang out of an over-refining on the

---

* "Now purgatory (as Bellarmine describeth it) is a certain place, in which, as in a prison-house, those souls are purged after this life, which were not fully purged in this life; that being so purged, they may be able to enter into heaven, whereinto no unclean thing can enter."— *Archbishop Usher*. There is not a word said of any purging of sins after death, in the paper of Karinus. That doctrine belongs legitimately to a later *development*, very natural, but very erroneous.

text of Scripture, if not from the baser source of inventing methods for rendering the laws of piety more acceptable to the passions of men. Thus purgatory, if it can make an offer at a Scriptural origin, becomes plainly, a straining of the statement of St. Paul, that at the day of judgment there will be some who have builded their works of 'hay, straw and stubble.' Such builders, are all the manufacturers of theories like this of purgatory. A great flame will their learned pages make, forsooth ! Or as we track it to a later age, it is plain that the strictness of the rules of evangelic piety was too great for the convenience of sinners and half-converted savages. Hence purgatory allowed a half-way house, where the difficulty could be met. The robber-king or noble on his death-bed, moved by terror of violated law, as frightful memories of murdered men and violated morals thronged around his bed, gave up his ill-gotten wealth and poured it at the foot of Holy

Church, to build houses for refuge against other robbers like himself. Did not Jesus forgive the thief on the cross? Will He not also condone these? But how? If there had been no middle state, to terrify the living sinners, they would look to a similar escape after their crimes, and throw off all fear. So in that strange life óf the Middle Ages, which we can hardly imagine, purgatory, with its grisly horrors, sent midnight dreams to the castles and donjons of the restless nobles and remorseless tyrants; and kept alive a fear in hearts, which were almost as hard as the stone-walls, which repelled all other foes. And it passed away with such ages. It is now mostly a thing of the past.

This early document has nothing of it, for neither the logic to pervert Scripture had yet arisen in the Church ; nor had the luxury of a later day invaded and softened its rigid, ascetic tone. Men living under the storms of pagan persecution, were more inclined to make a semi-purgatory of this world : as did Paul the Hermit or St. Anthony and the crowds of monks, wild as goblins in their fierce self-abnegation, who peopled the shores of the Nubian Nile. The writer of this story was a simple dreamer, who has told his belief, of things gained mostly by the myths and traditions of his age: myths in one view as imaginary as the Pilgrim's Progress; in another as *true*, being an allegory suited to all men and times. This dream tallies with both the Old and New Testament.

1. In the Old Testament the souls and bodies of men go, the one to the Underworld, the other to the dust. *Sheol*, for which Hebrew word came *Hades*, in the Greek translation, which was adopted into the New Testament, was a huge chasm or underground vault, not much unlike some of the royal tombs, only that it was immensely vast and shaded with a gloomy twilight, where the souls or shades of men, good and bad, were

confined, pale, tenuous, ghostly; a world where all things are forgotten, where there was no work and no device. This vast abode of the *Manes* or shades of all men, can be tracked through the entire Old Testament. Its origin was doubtless the old natural fancies, shown to have been even pre-historic. They passed to the Greeks and Romans, and are common more or less to all nations. Our English translation confuses us by calling two separate regions by the one name—Hell : 1, Hades, the place of imperfect rest, and *2*, *Gehenna*,* the place of final fire and destruction. The soul of David goes to *Sheol*—the soul of Jesus to Hades. It was the common theory and language; and without a special

---

* Hades occurs in the New Testament eleven times, Gehenna twelve times, and Tartarus once ; but in English all are called *hell;* though the souls of David and Jesus are both spoken of as in Hades (*Acts* ii. 27, 31), and Hades is said to be cast *into the lake of fire* at last (*Rev.* xx. 13, 14). Hades is once translated correctly, " O *grave,* where is thy victory?"—1 *Cor.* xv. 55.

revelation, there could have been no other theory. Granting death, and an immortal part, and a merciful God, and no more; and the soul or immortal part goes to some receptacle, which would be most likely to receive its chief characters, from what is seen to happen to the body; modified in some respects by the great natural scenery around, and the funeral customs of the age.

Up to the day of the resurrection of Jesus, this ideal Sheol or Hades was conqueror and ruler over the race of Adam. A twin to Death, he claimed all men for his own; dragging them down the valley of death-shade and feeding on them there.—See *Ecclesiastes* iii. 22.

One thing deserves careful consideration. The scenery of the Future is a reflection in advance of us, of the usages and ideas of the present. We say the *scenery*, not the underlieing facts. These latter abide; namely, a yearning for another life, and a protest against nothing-

ness : a desire to see the full compensation of the disappointments of this world;
a kindled spark of that "first deathless
fire" that tells of God the Father, to
whom it tends.   But the scenery is as
the image of the Brocken in the Hartz
Mountains ; a gigantic shadow in the
bright mist before us of what we are now.

The Pagan classic and the half-taught
Jew stood looking *down:* and far below the
surface he saw a realm of shadows, with
the lofty walls of the palace-prison of
Dis, and fiery Phlegethon on the one side ;
and the Elysian Meads on the other.
The Jews idealized Tophet from the
gloomy vale of the sons of Hinnom for
the bad : and told of Abraham's bosom,
of a lost Eden, and the space beneath the
Throne as the resting-places of the good.

Now, we bury our dead, and speak of
the great High Priest; of the Lamb; of the
New City and Paradise—not as below,
but all above, where in the Second
heaven the saints make a platform of the

clouds which shine resplendent with rainbow-colors. There is no Space for Spirit, say the metaphysicians. Perhaps so. Let us by this rule, so place them, that they be not too far removed from us. Just now we rear the marble memorials over their graves by thousands. We deck the sod with flowers, and hide all that is unsightly. Why, if not to claim them as nearer to us; to refuse to give them up so utterly as we have done; to people the cool retreats of the cemetery with their airy shades, and embrace them with our sympathies.

"They live whom we call dead."

They do not live myriad of Jupiter-orbits away from us; nor so absolute, as to have nothing now, in common with us. They live not in the gloomy, hot prison of mediæval torments—but near our hearts and in our loves and hopes, one with us in Christ's covenant.

2. Christ went and preached to the spirits in prison, *i. e.*, "*heralded* to the

souls *under guard.*" We need not dispute
over the theories of scholars on these
words, as they are mostly mere *devices,*
which do not bear any sifting. There
surely was something on St. Peter's mind,
which was told to spirits in the under-
world. Christ, when His soul fled from
Calvary, went whither all other souls went
before Him—went into Hades, as St.
Peter testifies, from the Psalm of David ;*
went to Paradise, as He Himself said to
the dying thief; as the creed words it in
all the ages, "descended into Hell," as
our rubric explains it, "the place of
departed spirits."

It is quite witty to ask, by way of ob-
jection, (only unfortunately the wit falls
like a mill stone on the author of it,)
"What did Jesus preach, if there were no
sinners to be converted?" We might
ask in return, what did He not preach to
those spirits who had waited since the
days of Noah. Fancy it. Say, for ex-

* *Acts* ii. 27, 31.

ample, that one who had refused Noah's call to enter his ark (what if multitudes had accepted it?) during that long, fatal storm, had repented? was there no room for a single change? Did an adamantine hardness shut down on all men, as God closed the door on the eight tremblers, hidden in the ark? Was the work then only a great, remorseless cataclysm and crush of death? Were there no human yearnings thereafter? If one man or boy repented of his error and died, then follow that soul, and see if there was not somewhere a message or word of mercy due him from the great Father who "made and loveth all." If, as Karinus wrote, their faculties were all complete, but they did not recognize each other, till that *luminousness* came stealing into Sheol, then, what did not such an old-world soul wish to know? Remember that there was no *covenant* on the earth when he died; and that St. Paul reasoned, that, where there was no law,

there was in some sense no transgression.
That soul which had lived before Abraham, knew very little on which to act by
faith in Christ. Was there nothing of
a Messiah to be told to it? As he came
to full consciousness, was there not a
need to hear that Christ had died: that
the blood of the Lamb of God cleansed
all, who had ever had grace to repent?
Is it not easier to invent reasons for Jesus
to go to those souls, than to keep Him
back from it? He went and *heralded*
news of jubilee to the long line of the
departed, from Adam to aged Simeon;
and in some special manner, "to those
which sometime were disobedient, when
once the long suffering of God waited in
the days of Noah while the Ark was a
preparing."—*1 Pet.* iii. 20.

What more natural scenery can we
have, than that of this ancient legend,
which has not a hint of Purgatory in it?
Certainly we may accept it if we add to
it one thing more, as the work which

Jesus accomplished in going to the spirits in prison.

3. He took them with Him to an upper world. Distinguish, reader, between the condition of man *before the last Judgment* and *after it ;* and possibly some perplexities may vanish. Before the Judgment the dead are without bodies, *natural or spiritual* (see 1 Cor. xv. 44, 52–54) ; and they are *not yet judged* (Jude 6), and therefore, compared with the after conditions, they are *imperfect.* Now, we may use the word *heaven* of both states, if we choose, but the facts are the same. One word is used for two very different conditions. No ancient writer ever confuses these two states. That has been left to moderns.

St. Paul seems to have been granted a vision of Paradise *all through ;* and though he tells us of nothing that he saw in it, he did two things of important use for us all. 1. He went in the strength of that vision through all after trials undaunted,

showing us what power there is in such
a vision.   2. He led the way, and St.
John, who saw Paradise and also told
us what he saw, followed him, in lifting
the faith of the Church out of the older,
· Jewish idea.   From that time on, Paradise was not under the earth, but above
it.; not in the Third or Seventh Heaven
of absolute perfectness, but up *to the
Third;* wanting only the resurrection and
the judgment to open the pearly gates of
Life, that the saints may be presented to
the Father.   Read a word or two of St.
Paul's vision in **2** *Cor.* xii. 1–7.   He
was caught up *into* Paradise (v. 4), and
he was caught up *as far as to* (*eos*) the
third heaven ; not *into* it, but up to it
(v. 3).   The matter of criticism apart,
the Christian no longer looks down to
Sheol to think of the departed, but up
to a Paradise, and a holy city, and an
inner holy place, or *Sanctum Sanctorum,*
within the veil, where there is no sun nor
moon, for they are not wanted; but where

is the very echo and conic curve of all
that is conceivable of joy and felicity : in
dissolving scenes, with now a city of
gems and perfectness, and now a river of
God gliding over golden sands and cher-
ishing the twelve-fruited tree which Adam
forgot to value, and now a vail falling before the ark of the law and its four-sided
cherubim with their chant unending of
Trisagion, and with thrones and angels
attendant, and crowned martyrs : as sweet
a dream ; as exalting to the faithful
soul, as man has or ever can have.
"Eye hath not seen," said the Jewish
prophet. Yea, responded St. Paul, but
the Spirit *hath* revealed them to us. It is
in this angle of the spheres, where all is
holy and full of the music of God, that
we find our paradise ; and wait the time,
when Jesus shall give up His golden
sceptre, and lay His crown at the feet of
the Father ; and God shall be all in all.
We fancy that a gloom would be lifted
from the grave, if we can realize that

Jesus has 'preached to the spirits in prison,' and muse on what that sermon might have been. If one could drop millenarian dreams from the last book of the Bible, and look on it as a revelation of the 'powers of the world to come' to us, between death and the resurrection, we might find a greater joy and peace in believing. They are the visions to pass over us as we rest in the grave, great waves of light and blessing, rippling into the narrow bays of our quiet cemeteries and churches and murmuring of the last and perfect state after the Day of Judgment, when death shall be swallowed up of life: and then cometh the victory and the final shout, 'O ! death, where is thy sting ! O Hades, where thy victory !'

> " Father, perfect my trust !
> Strengthen my feeble faith,
> Let me feel as I would when I stand
> On the shore of the river of Death.

> " Feel as I would, when my feet
> Are slipping over the brink ;
> For it may be I'm nearer home,
> Nearer than I think."

Easter Day.

March 28.   True Era, A.D. 28.

"Shall never* die."—*St. John* xi. 26.

Its golden gates swing inward noiselessly, .
Unlocked by silent fingers :
And while they stand a moment half ajar,
Gleams from the inner glory
Stream brightly through the azure vault afar,
And half reveal the story."

THE spectrum analysis shows us a strange fact or series of facts, of the element of light, which may be used with advantage to indicate certain lines of thought, concerning the great mystery of the resurrection, in which Christ brought

---

* The words of the Collect in the Burial Service " shall not *die eternally*," do not express the full force of the Greek *eis ton aiona*. See John iv. 14. There is a deeper sense, which is as true, that a soul touched by the blood of Christ beats with an impulse that abolishes death itself.

" life and immortality to light." One sees
in his darkened room or camera the single
ray which comes streaming in through a
minute orifice in the window, as it marks
its slanting track through the space by
the fine floating dust of the atmosphere.
The ray strikes on the prism, and its
parts cross and divide into the strange
beauty of varied colors. Here learned
men stopped for a time in their investiga-
tion. Then we learn that on each side
of the spectrum, as seen by the eye, there
are invisible rays as real as those which
we see. These have peculiar characters,
some almost mystical. On the side of
the red color, the invisible rays of *heat*
rise in intensity, into what Tyndall calls
a ' perfect Matter-horn ' of vigor. We
cannot see them until they are brought to
a focus, and some foreign substance inter-
posed. And on the violet side, beyond
the line where the eye stops, there are
stranger laws still. A solution of Quinia
is brushed over the dark wall, and in-

stantly a ghostly-gray light gleams on us, wavering and intermitting with half phosphoric sensitiveness, as if unwilling to be thus forcibly revealed; so that the observer feels a half dread, as if in thus intruding into the region of *actinic* rays, he were touching the confines of the ineffable. The explanation which science offers us of all this, is that the human eye is (in mercy) confined in its range to the narrow scale of the visible spectrum, and can see only rays of certain rapidities of vibration ; that what are beyond this scale are invisible, or made visible only by being hastened or retarded in their motion.

If this be so, is it too much to demand of others to think, and to speak oneself, only by a somewhat similar rule of thought, concerning certain religious subjects : that the human mind (in mercy to it) is confined by its own laws to a series of vital truths, of exquisite variety and beauty, now *white* and clear in a unit of light, and again dissected into seven-fold,

intermingling and yet distinct rays : and
no less that on both sides, or rather on
all sides, we reach out and up into divine
mysteries, the half of which we may see,
and the other half accept only by faith.
On the one hand, a Church vitalized by
the spirit of love and heat, focalizes into
miracles of grace, and mountains of
prejudice and hatred go down under the
invisible heat, as the ice and snow of the
glaciers melt (we know) more rapidly
from the *invisible* heat of the sun. And
on the violet side of Christian truth these
few chapters of the New Testament, that
tell of the resurrection of Jesus, hang
before us, and a form like unto the Son
of Man gleams before the eye of the
saint. It walked before the disciples,
not a ghost, yet passing strange. It
vanished up through the azure skies. It
appeared in light "exceeding magnifi-
cal" to Saul of Tarsus near Damascus ;
comforted St. John on the shore of Patmos. It is seen as it passes through

among the golden candlesticks; sits en-
throned in the temple; rides the White
Horse to universal conquest; stands in
the midst of the multitudes chanting their
hallelujahs, and is seen in the Paradise
restored, as in spotless white. It is the
light of the City which hath no need of
the sun nor moon; a mystery put in
words, half-held, half too grand and
intense to be more than believed—*a
spiritual body.* Not a spirit all or only,
not a body only, 'for flesh and blood
cannot inherit this kingdom.' The rays
of light have crossed, as in a lens, and
the two things known here, soul and
body, have passed into a new relation—a
tertium quid—the body of the *resurrection.* *

---

* "The flesh shall then be spiritual and subject to the
spirit, but still flesh, not spirit, as the spirit itself when
subject to the flesh, was fleshly, but still spirit and not
flesh." —— "but even in his body he will be spiritual,
when the same flesh shall have had that resurrection of
which these words speak." "But what this spiritual body
shall be, or how great its grace, I fear it were but rash to
pronounce, seeing that we have as yet no experience of it."
    St. Augustine's City of God, Book xxii. c. 21.

First let us follow our Lord 'this first-
born from the dead'—called *first-born*, for
others are to follow.   He appears first to
Mary of Magdala.   Two bands of women
set out to perfect the hasty work of Saturday.   One party of three, the Marys
and Salome, come first, starting before
dawn, and 'see the stone rolled away, and
a white messenger sitting on it, with
strangest words to them ; and they flee
amazed and terrified away.   The other
company come next, not meeting either
of them.

Mary of Magdala goes to Peter and
John, with the news of the vacant tomb,
and they run to the sepulchre.   It is now
day, and *a working day*, not a day of
rest, as with us.   Meanwhile, as Mary is
weeping at the sepulchre, she sees two
angels, who stand, as the cherubim did
over the mercy-seat, beneath which was
the Law.   So these, 'one at the head
and the other at the feet, where the body
of Jesus lay,' were doubtless heard by

the celestials, as afterwards by St. John, chanting 'Holy! Holy! Holy!'*

She turns back, and suddenly Jesus appears, a stranger (as He always does now to *no-faith*), and not recognized by her as her Lord. Love only can see Him now.† "Seeing, ye see not; hearing ye hear not." Her love for the dead Christ is shown; and to that the seeming gardener says, with the tone that has no error in it: "Mary!" and her Lord stands revealed before her. Something of earthly love mingled in the grateful heart of this woman, and she is not allowed to touch Him. Just after this, He meets the larger company, and they bow and salute Him without rebuke. The women then apparently go in one company and tell these events to the

---

* The cherubim are *silent* in the Old Testament—*vocal* in the New. Emblems of Nature and Science, they kept the way to the Tree, but did not tell it.

† Jesus was not visible to any unbeliever. The soldiers do not say that they saw Him. They saw too much else to think of that. At Emmaus, the two disciples did not *see* Him, until they began to thrill with loving faith.

disciples. Strange is the style of the record. Numberless are the questions we would fain ask. 'Did Jesus leave them? How did He disappear? Why did they not ask Him to go with them? Where were the disciples?' &c. But who *can* read these accounts and not see that he is walking in mystery? You perceive all the while a half-terror in all that the disciples do. There is a mingling of the human and super-human, in a gleaming *actinic* light, which tells of a profound law in the very revelation itself of 'thus far and no farther.' One may chill himself into denial, but, if he accept the record as authentic, it must be with a word to his unsanctified reason, saying : "*Here* shall thy proud waves be stayed."

Where the disciples of Jesus remained after the crucifixion, or under what general intention they kept together, we can have no idea. The words of the women "seemed to them as idle tales, and they believed them not." The news only

ended in "making them astonished."
For it seems that the *men* saw only the
vacant tomb and *"as yet they knew not the
Scriptures*, that He must rise again from
the dead." "If they believe not Moses
and the prophets neither will they believe
though one rose from the dead." It is
then for this day a woman's tale only.
Love has been vouchsafed the vision ; but
proud minds, reasoning, critical *men*, are
standing with the Scriptures in their hands,.
and 'as yet they believe not.'

Two disciples go to Emmaus in the
afternoon, one of them Cleophas. They
overtake a traveller, and their hearts burn
within them by the way, as 'He opened
the Scriptures,' beginning at Moses and
all the prophets, and showing them the
"open secret" of it all. Then, as an
act of 'breaking of bread with blessing'
touched the deep fountains of the heart,
their eyes were opened, and the *actinic ray*
struck on them, and they knew Him as
He vanished out of their sight. They

now, 'believing the Scriptures,' and so able in the use of love to see Him, hasten back to Jerusalem to tell the wondrous story. On reaching it they meet a new confirmation. "The Lord is risen indeed and hath appeared unto Simon," and they tell how He was known to them 'in the breaking of bread.' The doors were shut for fear of the Jews, when suddenly 'Jesus Himself stood in the midst of them.' Faith and sight, mystery and knowledge move together.

Jesus declares Himself to them, as a true man. "Handle Me and see, for a spirit hath not flesh and bones as ye see Me have." He eats before them. It is Himself. The tomb is vacant. His risen body is before them.

He shows them His hands and feet; and, on the next Sunday, He causes one of them to put his hand into the open wound in His side. He is not a body of such laws as ours, for the wound would have been a mortal one. No merely natural body could live by our laws, thus rent by the soldier's spear. We are thus led to both sides of the *spectrum*, or *thing seen*, to see what He is not : and faith accepts the contents of all that lies between those two *nots*. One *not* is, He was not a ghost or spirit only. The other *not* is, He was not a body of such laws as ours are. The thought between these two is given by St. Paul. It is the great, mystic creed of the Church to the end of all things.

"There is a *natural body* :" * that we have now, "first that which is natural." "The first Adam (or man) was made a living soul." He was—we are, "the earthy." "Flesh and blood cannot inherit the kingdom of God." The kingdom of God is *the Church*, here and hereafter. "And there is a *spiritual body*."†

---

* 1 Cor. xv. 44-58.

† "How is it that fumes of controversy still darken so clear a light? The Apostle distinctly tells you, that although the body is dead because of sin within you, yet even your mortal bodies shall be made alive because of

"Afterward that which is spiritual."
"The last Adam was made a *life-giving*
Spirit." He is, we are *becoming*, "the
heavenly." "Lo! I show you a mystery:
we shall not all sleep, but we shall *all be
changed.*" This mortal will put on immortality. The soul was immortal before:
it drops the corruptible, mortal part, and
puts on its *building of God* not made with
hands, eternal in the heavens.

One is tempted to stop here and refer
the questioner to the poet's fancy, which
may be the sweetest rebuke to a cold
doubt: premising only, that St. Paul's
argument began in the seed; in one
seed, dying, and from its germ, as it died,
wheat springing as 'God hath given it a

---

righteousness, by reason of which even now your spirit is
life,—the whole of which process is to be perfected by the
grace of Christ, in other words, by His Spirit that dwell-
eth in you. Well, do men still gainsay? He goes on to
tell us how this comes to pass, how that life converts
death into itself, by mortifying it: that is, the spirit of life,
by mortifying the body, renders it spiritual and full of
life."—*St. Augustine, De Peccatorum, etc., Lib. I. cap.*
vii.

body ;' and ends with 'Star differeth from
star in glory.' Shall not the two bodies
of man; the one decaying and the other
indestructible, differ too? But one thinks
of Adam on that first day of Eden, as the
night came down on nature and hid the
landscape and the flowers, in one universal black pall, to ask—

> "Did he not tremble for this lovely frame?
> Hesperus with the host of heaven came,
> And lo! creation widened in man's view.
> Who could have thought *such darkness lay concealed
> Within thy beams, O Sun!* Or who could find,
> While fly, and leaf, and insect stood revealed,
> That to such countless orbs thou mad'st us blind?
> *Why do we then shun death* with anxious strife?
> If light can thus deceive, *wherefore not life?"*
>
> BLANCO WHITE.

We turn our eyes on the little beam
which comes to us, through the crack of
our drawn blinds, and muse in wonder
over all which we know it hides: or as we
open its secrets, by the help of science,
we learn to be modest at that spiritual
ray, which came down to us through
the "Gates ajar." And as our infants
sing, we may join them in saying:

"Now never a sad-eyed mother
But may catch the glory afar,
Since safe in the dear Christ's bosom
Are the keys of the gates ajar;
Close hid in the dear Christ's bosom;
And the gates forever ajar!"
From the Italian.

And now, reader, ere we part, and this
Holy Week passes into the record of our
lives; and its influences drop into the
'hearts' deep well,' as one more 'practice'
of the Song of the Redeemed; one more
great, annual effort to stand on the height
of our Churchly life and reach up higher
to see the vision of the 'angels ascend-
ing and descending on the Son of Man,'
(which vision Jacob declared to be the
'very gate of heaven' opening to him,)
let us lay these thoughts to heart. You
may question them, if you will, in some
of their minutiæ, but at least try them
carefully, and use them as the *key* to the
'Gates ajar' to you. You note that the
disciples did not see the Lord; 'for as
yet they believed not the Scriptures.'
Do you? You note that they did catch

the first start and impetus of faith, in the act of Love, namely, in the breaking of Bread with blessing. May not you? Why should not Emmaus have its lesson; that, in that rite, which symbolizes all love and intercommunion on the one side, and all mystic teaching of priest and prophet, of evangel and epistle on the other, to show Christ's death—it may show Him to be no longer dead, but alive unto God!

But these now are our last words together; and if we meet on that upper shore of the river of Life, may they have given you such spiritual help as they have often the writer.

I. There are two states of the future not to be rashly confused—the state before the Judgment, and the state after the Judgment. We now call both of them by the one word—*heaven*, and do thus confuse them. We say of the dead—they are gone to heaven, and stop there.

But surely a bodiless soul, and a mysti-
cally embodied soul *are not the same* in
all things. A soul judged, and unjudged,
are not in one and the same state.

My own belief is, that the revelation of
the after-judgment condition is that ineffable truth, which has never yet been
spoken ; while the time after death up
to the Judgment, is that covered by the
words of holy writ. We are permitted to
know what the joys of the souls in Paradise are now, while they wander in
Elysian meads, and wait for the Bride-
groom's midnight call. What things
God hath prepared beyond the Resurrection and the Judgment, pass all understanding.

The language of Scripture seems to
land the redeemed race finally in one
great crisis : when the Conqueror over
Death, 'the last enemy that shall be destroyed,' having finished His work, shall
then surrender His sceptre over the
world and be subject unto the Father, who

put all things under Him, that God may
be all in all (1 *Cor.* xv. 27). Till then,
Christ is the only One of all mankind
who has risen from the dead in a spiritual
body, to the right hand of God.

II. If this be so, then the language of
Scripture as to our future life, belongs
strictly to *disembodied souls.* Paradise, as
we saw in a former chapter, was lifted out
of the Under-world, and put below the
Third Heaven—neither below us, under
the surface, as it had been before, nor yet
too far for us to reach to it. St. John
has given us plain marks by which to
know this fact. 1. He saw the new
heaven and new earth, where all tears are
washed away ; and lo ! it is the Church
which he saw and not the after-judgment
state—for it was the Bride, the Lamb's
wife—the Holy City,

> " Whose ageless walls are bonded
> With amethyst unpriced,
> The saints make up the fabric,
> And the corner-stone is Christ."

'Yea,' says one, 'the Church of the

future.' Nay, but he says : "The nations of them that are saved (*sozomenon*,
of those, now being saved) do bring their
glory and their honor into it." They do
it now. There are no such nations beyond the Judgment.

2. He saw Paradise regained by man.
It is a dissolving view: for it is part
Eden, and part a city (*Rev.* xxii. 2),
and no Cherubim are seen longer to
guard the gate. They are now within;
and are heard chanting near the throne.
Again the Tree of Life comes into view,
and it is not *future*, but *now :* "the leaves
of the Tree are for the healing of the
nations." No nations remain after the
'earth and the worlds are burned up,'
to be healed by it. Almost all Christians
have learned from the old Catholic poetry,
to apply all such language in sacred song
to the Intermediate state. Why not
in plain prose? and meet death, as

> "but a covered way
> Which opens *into light :*
> Wherein no blinded child can stray
> Beyond the Father's sight."

Surely we lose the power of the sublimest consolations of Scripture, by confusing these two futures. Take the two thoughts : of one future of disembodied souls in joy and felicity, up to that great Easter, and see how all joyful images spring up around the silent realm of spirits. Then ponder the grand silence of Scripture—of our last great 'bridal of earth and sky '—where perfected manhood in Christ is borne far above all angels and principalities and powers in heavenly places, to be presented to the Infinite as a Bride, a consummate ideal and acme of all conceivable worth, fit for the love of the Infinite.

III. And so, finally, we come to the full meaning of the Easter Chant—of a moral resurrection : of eternal life begun here on earth: "Likewise reckon ye yourselves to be dead indeed *unto sin,* but alive unto God, through Christ our Lord." We look back over the Past as one

long Passion Week—its early covenants,
'the like figures whereunto,' scattered
along its path, from the early dawn,
when Abraham kept guard over the vic-
tims till the sun went down; through Israel's darkness and Passover; along the line
of the ages, to where Christ taught us that
the first Covenant was intended to make
way for the Second Covenant, by which He
came *to do God's will ;* and by that doing
sanctify us to do the same. We see the
temple cleansed of avarice as a type for
each one of us. We hear all the words
of the true wisdom as spoken to us, and
obey them. In simple love we escape
the treachery of mere blind knowledge,
and are taught by the Saviour's humble
deed of mercy. We cleanse the heart to
receive the ' Bread of heaven ;' and learn
to give God, in our way, our dearest
thing—even every idol and passion ; and
learn to die in faith, knowing that in
some true, depth of thought, "he that
liveth and believeth in Christ, shall never

die." Death is only transition. It opens Paradise : and we are only passing out of the shadow into the sun. And for others who have gone ; yea, for ourselves who are soon to go, we can say,

"Heaven is but life made richer ; therein can be no loss :
 We breathe one air, beloved, we follow one dear Guide :
 Passed into open vision, out of our mist and rain,
 Ye see how sorrow blossoms, how peace is won from pain :
 No adamant between us uprears its rocky screen !
 A veil before us only—Ye in the light serene."

LUCY LARCOM.

Our Lord has once solemnly set the lines of this spectrum in the camera of His open tomb.

1. There is a moral resurrection, the Seed of the other. "Verily, verily I say unto you, He that heareth my word, and believeth on Him that sent Me, *hath* (not shall have, but *has it now*) everlasting life, and shall not come into condemnation ; but *is passed* from death unto life. Verily, verily I say unto you, the hour is coming *and now is* (it was not future, but was there and then) when the dead shall hear the

voice of the Son of God, and they that
hear shall live.   These are the dead in sin.
(Three thousand of such heard it on the
day of Pentecost, and myriads have done
so since.) ''For as the Father hath life in
Himself, so hath He given to the Son to
have life in Himself" (and to impart it).

2. There is a resurrection of the dull
body unto spiritual life, after the soul has
quickened it with faith in the glory of
God.   '' Marvel not at this, for the hour
is coming (not and now is, but left to the
far future and undetermined) in the
which all that are in the graves shall hear
His voice and shall come forth; they
that have done good unto the resurrection
of life : and they that have done evil unto
the resurrection of damnation." Let us
rise now from all sin and evil, that we
may pass now from death to life ; to wait
in Paradise for the next great Easter, when
at His call the Bride of Christ shall rise
without spot or wrinkle or any such thing.

" Oh Heart, what helps it to adore
   His cradle where the sunrise glows ?
Or what avail to kneel before
   The Grave whence long ago He rose ?
That He should find in thee a birth,
   That thou shouldest seek to die to earth
And live to Him ; —— this, this must be
   Thy Bethlehem and Calvary !"

FRIEDRICH RÜCKERT.